P9-BZQ-786

MONSTER ✚ HIGH

MONSTER RESCUE
I SPY DEUCE GORGON!

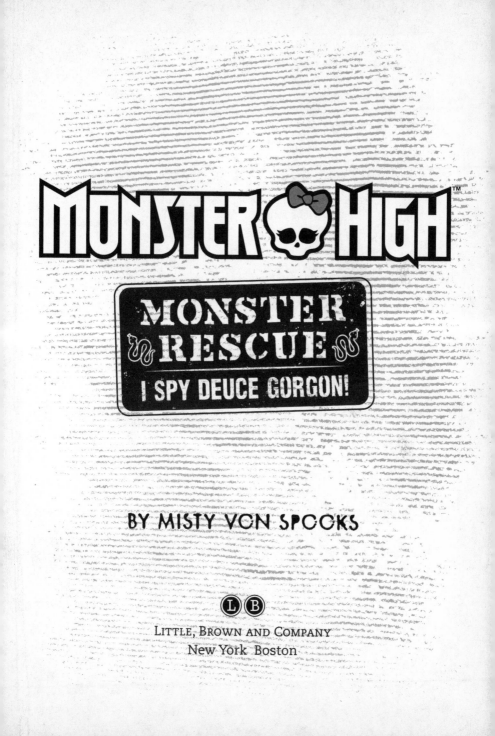

MONSTER HIGH™

MONSTER RESCUE

I SPY DEUCE GORGON!

BY MISTY VON SPOOKS

Ⓛ Ⓑ

LITTLE, BROWN AND COMPANY
New York Boston

This book is a work of fiction. Names, characters, places, and incidents are the product of the author's imagination or are used fictitiously. Any resemblance to actual events, locales, or persons, living or dead, is coincidental.

MONSTER HIGH and associated trademarks are owned by and used under license from Mattel. © 2018 Mattel. All Rights Reserved.

Cover design by Véronique Lefèvre Sweet.
Cover illustration by Yulia Rumyantseva.

Hachette Book Group supports the right to free expression and the value of copyright. The purpose of copyright is to encourage writers and artists to produce the creative works that enrich our culture.

The scanning, uploading, and distribution of this book without permission is a theft of the author's intellectual property. If you would like permission to use material from the book (other than for review purposes), please contact permissions@hbgusa.com. Thank you for your support of the author's rights.

Little, Brown and Company
Hachette Book Group
1290 Avenue of the Americas, New York, NY 10104
Visit us at LBYR.com
Visit monsterhigh.com

First Edition: January 2018

Little, Brown and Company is a division of Hachette Book Group, Inc. The Little, Brown name and logo are trademarks of Hachette Book Group, Inc.

The publisher is not responsible for websites (or their content) that are not owned by the publisher.

Library of Congress Control Number 2017955140

ISBNs: 978-0-316-55791-7 (paper over board), 978-0-316-55794-8 (ebook)

Printed in the United States of America

LSC-H

10 9 8 7 6 5 4 3 2 1

MONSTER HIGH™

MONSTER
RESCUE
I SPY DEUCE GORGON!

CHAPTER 1

Cleo de Nile groaned as she pulled her shiny black-and-gold hair over her face. "I can't go on," she said, her voice muffled by the curtain of hair.

"Come on, ghoul, it's not that bad!" Draculaura said encouragingly. "We're at *least* halfway done with our lab assignment...or, maybe, thirty percent...or I guess a quarter done is more accurate..."

Cleo groaned again. "I'm going to need a Mummy Mocha before I can do anything else," she said.

"Let's just do a little more, and then we can take a break," Draculaura replied. She glanced down at the assignment and carefully read, "'As you explore the differences between refraction and reflection, calculate the angle of incidence and the angle of reflection.'"

"It's like you're speaking some made-up language," Cleo said. "What does any of that even mean?"

"I think that's why we're supposed to do the assignment," Draculaura said, trying not to giggle. "So we can understand whatever it means." But Cleo sighed even more dramatically, blowing her hair out of her face. Cleo's pained expression was reflected in the glossy chrome of Monster High's Mad Science lab, a state-of-the-art laboratory deep under the school.

Draculaura couldn't blame Cleo for wanting to take a break. It was a ghoulgeous Saturday, and most of their classmates at Monster High were enjoying the freedom of the weekend. She could just picture them hanging out on the lawn, relaxing by the saltwater pool, or chilling in the common rooms...Draculaura and Cleo would've loved to join them, but all their extracurricular activities during the week meant that weekends were the only time they could work on their lab project together.

Monster High hadn't always been a school. Not that long ago, it was a house—well, actually, more like an enormous mansion, where Draculaura and her dad, Dracula, lived in complete and total seclusion. Ever since the great monster Fright Flight, *all* monsters lived that way—alone, hidden, stuck in the shadows. Sure, Draculaura loved her dad and her pet spider, Webby, but after a few hundred years living in hiding, she couldn't shake the loneliness—or the sense that somewhere out there, other monsters longed for monster friends just as much as she did.

That's when Draculaura had her most fang-tastic idea ever: Monster High. She dreamed of a place where monsters could live and learn in peace until humans could accept them. They'd have the opportunity to be together and to experience everything they'd been missing since they'd gone into hiding! And Draculaura couldn't think of a better place than the enormous mansion she and her dad shared.

Of course, their house needed a few improvements and upgrades. However, the big challenge was finding all those hidden monsters that Draculaura was convinced were out there. Frankie Stein, the first student to arrive, spotted Draculaura during one of her flying lessons. And Clawdeen Wolf was easy to locate when the ghouls prowled around the nearby moor. But Draculaura knew that there were monsters all around the globe who should have the opportunity to attend Monster High too. Once she sent a message to them on the Monster Web, the requests came pouring in—and after several exciting monster rescue missions, Monster High was finally up and running. It was a total dream come true!

"All right, Cleo." Draculaura finally gave in. "We'll take a quick Mummy Mocha break. We *have* been studying all morning. I think we've earned it!"

"Thanks, ghoulfriend," Cleo said gratefully.

As the ghouls walked through the lab, their footsteps echoed across the cold slate floor. The lab was so far under Monster High that none of the school's noise reached them; there were no windows, so it was impossible to know how much time had passed unless you were watching the clock. Which, Draculaura had to admit, Cleo often was! As the ghouls climbed the spiral staircase up to the main floor, Draculaura glanced at her iCoffin to check the time.

The screen was flashing with an alert. She had a new video message, which could mean only one thing.

A new monster wanted to come to Monster High!

CHAPTER 2

"Cleo!" Draculaura shrieked. "Look at this—a new video message!"

"Are you kidding me?" Cleo gasped. "Is that what I think it is?"

"I think so," Draculaura answered, grinning. "Sounds like we might need to plan another monster rescue mission!"

"Where do you think we'll go this time?" Cleo asked. "Do you think it'll be somewhere warm and sunny and covered in palm trees…Oh! Maybe with a spa?"

"I have no idea," Draculaura replied. "It could be anywhere in the whole wide world."

She was absolutely right. Their monster rescue missions had led them to Egypt to rescue Cleo, Australia to rescue Lagoona, and right down the street to rescue Twyla! There was no way to know where the next monster rescue would be—sometimes not even until the ghouls had departed Monster High. Luckily, the Monster Mapalogue always knew just where to take them.

"Do you know where everybody is?" Draculaura asked Cleo. "We can't watch the video message without our best ghoulfriends."

"No, of course not," Cleo quickly agreed. "I bet Lagoona's in the pool practicing her laps. And I think Frankie and Clawdeen are working on a project today."

"That's right!" Draculaura exclaimed. "They have that big history project due next week."

"I don't know, ghoul," Cleo said, pretending to frown. "There seems to be *a lot* of homework. Maybe you could do something about that? Like talk to your dad, aka *the principal?*"

Draculaura laughed. "Sorry, Cleo," she said. "I think homework is just a part of going to Monster High."

"I'm starting to get that." Cleo sighed. "I'll go hit the pool and get Lagoona—"

"And I'll find Clawdeen and Frankie," Draculaura finished. "I'm guessing they'll be in the Howl of History or the Libury."

"Meet you back at the Creepeteria," Cleo said. "There's a Mummy Mocha with my name on it!"

"And one with mine!" Draculaura added with a laugh. Then she hurried off to find Frankie and Cleo. She had a feeling that they'd be holed up

in the Howl of History, one of her favorite class-
rooms in Monster High. It was there that Draculaura had done research for the ghouls' very first
rescue mission—to free Cleo, who was trapped
in her tomb inside one of the great pyramids of
Egypt.

Along the way, Draculaura paused to say hi
and chat with several of her new classmates. She
grinned when she saw Twyla, a boogey-ghoul who
had lived just down the hill in the Boogey Mansion before they found her and brought her to the
school. That rescue had been trickier than Draculaura expected because Twyla was so shy that
she wasn't sure she even wanted to attend Monster High. But the appeal of the school eventually
won out, and Draculaura noticed that Twyla had
started to spend more and more time on campus.
And when Twyla's social time maxed out, she had
a knack for disappearing into her surroundings—
a trick Draculaura never tired of watching.

When Draculaura reached the Howl of History, she found Frankie and Clawdeen working closely together. Their heads were bent over an enormous, dusty book with ragged yellow pages.

"Ghouls!" Draculaura cried out eagerly. "Guess what?"

Clawdeen and Frankie were so engrossed in what they were reading that they didn't even notice when Draculaura came in. Her voice startled them so much that they knocked their heads together as they jumped. As their heads collided, sparks flew into the air.

"*Ahhhh!*" Frankie yelped, tightening one of the bolts in her neck.

"*Owwww!*" Clawdeen cried, rubbing her cheek. "I think your bolt sparked me!"

"Sorry," Frankie said, blushing. "I spark even more when I'm surprised."

"I'm sorry too," Draculaura added. "I didn't mean to startle you. It's just that I've got big news—no, *huge* news—no, make that *monstrously massive news!*"

"What is it?" Frankie and Clawdeen cried, which was the reaction Draculaura had expected.

Draculaura held up her iCoffin. "Just in," she said breathlessly. "A new video on the Monster Web!"

That was all Draculaura needed to say. From the way Frankie and Clawdeen squealed with excitement, she could tell that they knew exactly what she meant.

"Tell us *everything!*" Frankie exclaimed. "Who, what, when, where, *why—*"

Draculaura gave her a look. "Ghoul, you don't really think I'd watch a monster rescue request without you?" she replied. "Come on! Cleo and Lagoona are going to meet us at the Creepeteria."

"Voltageous," Frankie cheered. "We could use a Mummy Mocha break."

"How's the history project going?" asked Draculaura.

"It's *not* easy," Frankie replied. "We have to research monsters of yesteryear, then write a skit about them. I'd much rather be working on an experiment in the lab."

Draculaura thought about how little Cleo wanted to work on their science project and laughed. "Be careful what you wish for," she said. "Cleo would *strongly* disagree."

"So your science project's going that well, huh?" asked Clawdeen, stifling a laugh

"We'll get it done," Draculaura said with a sigh. "After all, we don't exactly have a choice."

"Too bad Cleo and I can't switch places," Frankie said wistfully. "With her flair for the dramatic, I bet she'd write a voltageous script for the history presentation."

"We can't do only what we're good at, though,"

Draculaura pointed out. "Monster High is all about broadening our horizons! Trying new things! Experiencing all the monster world has to offer!"

Clawdeen raised an eyebrow. "Have you been hanging out in the guidance counselor's office again?" she asked knowingly.

Draculaura giggled. "I may have helped with some filing yesterday," she replied.

"I thought so," Clawdeen teased her ghoulfriend. "Because you sound just like a motivational poster!"

"Draculaura's right, though," Frankie said. "If I wanted to spend my entire life in a lab, I could've just stayed home with my dad." Frankie's father, Dr. Frankenstein, loved experimenting as much as she did.

"And where would be the fun in that?" Draculaura replied. "Whoops! Sorry! Excuse me! Coming through!"

The corridors were crowded with monsters on

their way to the Creepeteria. "Is it that close to lunchtime?" Draculaura asked. "I hope there isn't a long line again."

"Bad news," Clawdeen reported, standing on tiptoe to peer over the crowd. "There is."

"Oh bats!" Draculaura groaned lightly. "Well, you know, at least all these new students seem to love the school! I'm so happy to see everyone settled and making friends and causing long lines in the Creepeteria…"

"Yeah, hopefully our ghoulfriends already snagged a spot in that line," added Clawdeen, craning her neck to search for them.

"We did even better than that," a new voice spoke up. Draculaura would've recognized the distinctive Australian accent anywhere. She spun around to see Lagoona Blue and Cleo standing near the entrance to the Creepeteria, holding a tray with five iced Mummy Mochas on it!

"Voltageous!" cheered Frankie.

"If only we could have nabbed a table too," Cleo said, glancing around the crowded Creepeteria.

"That's okay," Draculaura assured her. "We should probably find some place a little more... private to watch the video message."

The other ghouls exchanged a knowing look. They understood exactly what Draculaura meant. A new student at Monster High was a big deal, and if the others knew that Draculaura and her best ghouls were getting ready for another rescue mission, they would want *all* the details.

I can't believe it, Draculaura marveled as they climbed the spiral staircase to her bedroom in one of Monster High's tallest turrets. *It wasn't that long ago that I was terminally lonely, dreaming of escaping from my bedroom—and now I have to escape there just to get a little privacy!* Draculaura couldn't have been happier to have such a full school!

As soon as the ghouls reached Draculaura's bedroom, she closed the door firmly behind them.

The ghouls grabbed some oversize pink-and-black pillows and settled on the floor as Lagoona handed out their Mummy Mochas. Her long aqua-streaked hair was still damp from a morning of swim practice in Monster High's saltwater pool.

"How's the pool?" Draculaura asked her. "Is the salt concentration right?"

"Oh, it's fintastic!" Lagoona exclaimed. "I've got big news! Mr. D. finally agreed to sponsor Monster High's very first swim team! We have tryouts this afternoon!"

The other ghouls cheered so loudly that they woke Draculaura's pet spider, Webby, who was snoozing in the cobwebs over her bed.

"That's fangtastic!" Draculaura said.

"I'm so excited," Lagoona replied. "Of course, I've got to brush up myself. I'm still getting used to swimming in a pool, you know."

"It must be a lot different from swimming in the ocean," Draculaura responded. She wouldn't soon forget their dramatic rescue of Lagoona. The waters of the Great Barrier Reef had been brilliantly blue, clear, and calm—until a terrible typhoon hit, tossing Draculaura and her friends into the middle of the Outback! Draculaura wasn't sure she and her ghoulfriends would make it back to Monster High—let alone rescue Lagoona. But despite the dangers of the Outback and the wild unpredictability of the weather, their mission had been a success.

When all the ghouls were sipping their Mummy Mochas, Draculaura pulled up the video on her iCoffin. The other ghouls crowded around to watch on the tiny screen. A grainy image appeared of a manster—at least, Draculaura *thought* it was a manster, but it was hard to tell because whoever had sent the video had gone to great lengths to conceal his or her appearance. There was a hat pulled low on his head, and his hand shielded the top half of his face.

"Hey," a low voice said. "My name is Deuce. I'm from Greece."

So he is a manster, Draculaura thought.

"I, uh, I've been thinking about Monster High a lot," Deuce continued. "Like, practically nonstop."

"Join the club," Lagoona spoke up, making the other ghouls giggle.

"But I have to admit I'm also...not sure Monster High is right for me," Deuce said. He shifted uncomfortably. "I know it's for monsters and all but...some of my monster traits make it, uh, well, kind of hard to play well with others."

Draculaura had no idea what he meant—and from the baffled looks on her ghoulfriends' faces, neither did they.

"But I really want to go to Monster High," Deuce said, a sudden note of determination in his voice. "Do you think you could help me out?"

The screen went black. The video was over. Deuce's question seemed to hang in the air for a few moments. At last, Cleo broke the silence with a sigh.

"He. Is. So. *Cute!*" she said in a dreamy voice.

"How could you tell?" Frankie asked practically. "He was pretty much hiding his whole face."

"I just could," Cleo insisted. "Some people just have a certain *aura*."

"Why do you think he didn't want us to see him?" asked Draculaura.

Clawdeen's eyes grew wide. "Maybe he's surrounded by vicious Normies and trying to hide his true self until he can get to the safety of Monster High!" she exclaimed.

"Or," Cleo said loudly, "maybe he's *insanely* popular and has to go, like, incognito to avoid being mobbed by crowds of adoring ghouls!"

"Or maybe he's the sneaky type," Frankie suggested, narrowing her eyes dramatically. "You know. Sly and secretive."

"Or maybe it's just a habit," offered Draculaura.

"You know, from spending centuries hiding from Normies."

"Honestly?" Lagoona spoke up. "It was probably the sun. It looked *really* fierce. Bet it was shining right in his eyes."

"That makes sense," Draculaura said slowly. After all, Lagoona would know about the glare of fierce sun from her time in the Great Barrier Reef. Draculaura had been so preoccupied by Deuce's odd behavior that she hadn't even noticed his surroundings in the video.

"Does it even matter?" Cleo asked suddenly.

Everyone turned to look at her.

"I just mean...even if Deuce is secretive or surrounded by Normies or mobbed by fanghouls," she continued, "he's still welcome here—right?"

"Of course," Draculaura said firmly. "*Everyone* is welcome at Monster High!"

CHAPTER 3

Knock-knock-knock!

The sound of someone rapping on the door startled Draculaura. Surrounded by her best ghoulfriends, she wasn't expecting any visitors. She jumped up and hurried across the room.

"Dad!" she exclaimed when she swung open the door. "What are you doing here?"

Dracula raised an eyebrow at his only daughter and smiled. "Good to see you too," he teased.

"You know what I mean," Draculaura said, holding the door open wider. "Come on in."

"I see the gang's all here," Dracula said as he leaned against the wall. "How are your studies, ghouls?"

"Good," everyone chorused.

"Except those midsemester projects, though," Cleo spoke up. "Killer!"

Dracula's eyes twinkled with excitement. "Monster High is going to have a reputation for a grueling academic program," he said proudly. "Thanks to the efforts of our first class of students—and by that, I mean all of you!"

"Grueling—or gruesome?" Clawdeen joked.

"Or both!" Cleo laughed.

"We're just kidding, Mr. D.," Frankie said. "We know you're just making us the smartest ghouls we can be!" The other ghouls nodded in agreement, though a bit halfheartedly.

"Dad, we have some big news," Draculaura said, holding up her phone. "Looks like we've got a new monster rescue!"

"Really?" Dracula exclaimed. Draculaura couldn't tell if he was really surprised, or just trying to fake it. Somehow, her dad always seemed to show up right around when a new video or voice mail popped up on her iCoffin…as if, somehow, he knew about it before she even had a chance to tell him. Knowing her dad, of course, Draculaura wouldn't be a bit surprised if he did have some sort of secret monster knowledge. She had a feeling that when it came to monster history, lore, and powers, she still had a lot to learn.

"His name is Deuce, and he's from *Greece!*" Cleo said, almost breathlessly.

"Greece?" Dracula repeated. It was clear his interest was piqued—and so was his worry. "That country is legendary for its monsters and big beasties."

"Really?" asked Draculaura.

"Certainly," Dracula replied. "In fact, ancient Greece was chock-full of some of the most interesting monsters of all time! The Normies like to think that ancient Greek monsters are the stuff of long-ago myths and legends. Of course, they couldn't be more wrong."

Dracula's chuckle was contagious, and soon everyone was laughing with him. Normies could pose a serious risk to monsters—Draculaura knew that no one would ever forget the great monster Fright Flight—but it was pretty ridiculous that Normies believed monsters no longer existed!

"Greece is one of those places so steeped in history it's inescapable," Dracula continued. "Ghouls, don't even think of running off on another monster rescue there without some extensive research into ancient Greek history."

"*Extensive?*" Cleo echoed, looking crestfallen. "Exactly how extensive are we talking, Mr. D.?"

"Yeah," Draculaura added. "You know we hate to leave a monster in distress waiting, Dad."

"It could be *dangerous* in Greece, ghouls! And while *I* know that you're going to Greece to rescue this Deuce manster, the beasties there don't! So I think you need to start with at least some background research," Dracula said, clearing his throat and trying not to sound like too much of a worrywart. "In fact, I just happened to be passing through the Howl of History and I saw quite a few books left on the tables. If I'm not mistaken, I believe some of them covered this very topic."

Clawdeen and Frankie exchanged a guilty look. "That's our bad," Clawdeen spoke up. "We're working on a project about monsters from history."

"Actually, it was my fault," Draculaura chimed in. "I interrupted them with news of a new monster rescue mission."

"But you know we'll shelve *all* those books and clean everything up," Frankie said.

Dracula smiled at the ghouls. "That's the least of my concerns," he said. "Tidying should never get in the way of studying."

"Or rescue missions!" Draculaura added.

"Precisely. And you ghouls have *a lot* of research-ing ahead of you before you can Mapalogue out of here!" Dracula said with a mix of pride and anxi-ety. "Let me know if you need any help."

"Thanks, Dad," Draculaura said, holding up the Skullette charm that she wore around her neck and used to make the Monster Mapalogue work. "We will."

"Oh! And one more thing," Dracula said as he was halfway out the door. "Please remember to—"

"Be careful!" all the ghouls said at once before dissolving into giggles.

"You took the words right out of my mouth," Dracula said.

"Okay, ghouls! This is happening! It's really happening!" Draculaura said once her dad had disappeared down the hall. All this time, Draculaura had appreciated the break from monster rescues—but now that there was another one on the horizon, she couldn't hide her excitement. And her enthusiasm was infectious.

"You know the drill," Draculaura continued. "We'll tackle the research first. Frankie and Clawdeen, do you want to go back to the Howl of History? Learn all about the monsters we might encounter?"

"You got it, Draculaura," Clawdeen replied. "And we'll be cranking on our history project too. Double duty!"

Draculaura turned to Lagoona and Cleo. "How about we hit the Libury?" she asked. "We can research more about Greece—you know, the landscape, the terrain, all those things we need to know about a place before we, like, show up there."

"Sure," Cleo said. "I can't *wait* to learn all about

Deuce's home! He sounds almost as exotic and regal as *moi*!"

But Lagoona looked conflicted. "Um…ghouls…" she began.

"What's wrong?" Draculaura asked.

"It's just—today is a really, really bad day for me to take off on a rescue mission," she explained.

"Swim team tryouts!" Draculaura suddenly remembered. "How could I forget?"

Lagoona shrugged. "It's okay," she said. "I could try to reschedule them…"

But Draculaura shook her head. "You've worked really, *really* hard to get a swim team started at Monster High," she said. "I don't want to derail all your progress!"

"I really wish I could be in two places at once!" Lagoona groaned.

"That would take some seriously strong monster magic," Draculaura said. "I don't even know if it's possible. Let's research it!"

Lagoona's eyes lit up with excitement, and Draculaura dove into research on her iCoffin.

"Ghouls," Frankie spoke up, "I hate to state the obvious, but as much as I want to find a way around the space-time continuum, getting into that research will *definitely* delay Deuce's rescue mission."

Lagoona shook her head firmly. "No way, then," she declared. "That wouldn't be fair to Deuce."

"Would you be upset if we went on a rescue mission without you?" asked Draculaura.

"Of course not!" Lagoona exclaimed. "I mean, I'd be sorry to miss it…and I feel bad sticking you with all the work…but maybe it's good to keep one of us on at Monster High, and keep the swim tryouts on track."

It was a hard decision to make, but in the end, Draculaura could see there was only one choice. "Okay," she finally said. "If you're *sure*, then you're absolutely right! You should go rally up a creeper-ific swim team!"

"I will!" Lagoona said gratefully. "Thanks, ghouls. I hope I'm not letting you down."

"Definitely not," Frankie assured her.

"I can't wait to hear all about it!" Lagoona said, standing up. The rest of the ghouls rose too.

"Let's get ready for our rescue mission," Draculaura told the others. "Meet you in the Creepeteria in … what do you think? Two hours?"

"Sounds good," Clawdeen replied.

Cleo took a long sip of her Mummy Mocha. "I agree," she added. "And by then, I will *definitely* need a refill!"

CHAPTER 4

When Draculaura and Cleo arrived at the Libury, it was even quieter than usual. Draculaura had a feeling that the beautiful weather outside had played a part! It was nice to have practically the whole Libury to themselves—and to talk about their rescue mission without worrying that other monsters would overhear them.

"Let's see," Draculaura said as she scanned the shelves. "*Greece: Jewel of the Aegean. Isles of Myth and Mystery. Ancient Greece's Arts and Artifacts. Cradle of*

Culture. And that's just the start. There are way more books about Greece than I expected!"

"Great," Cleo said, trying (and failing) to sound enthusiastic. She knew being prepared was one of the most important parts of any rescue mission. But if she were completely honest, she'd rather get going than research the country of Greece.

Draculaura pulled a stack of books off the shelf and placed half in Cleo's arms. "Let's split up our sources. We'll cover the material twice as fast," she said.

At one of the long tables in the middle of the Libury, they both quietly worked their way through their stacks. Cleo flipped through a book without really reading any of the words. "What do you think Deuce meant?" she asked suddenly.

Draculaura, lost in her book, glanced up. "Huh?" she asked, confused.

"When this manster said that his monster

traits made it hard for him to get along with other monsters?" Cleo reminded her. "What do you think he meant by that?"

"Oh," Draculaura said thoughtfully. "I don't know. I guess we'll have to ask him when we see him."

Cleo sighed, unsatisfied with her friend's answer. Sure, they didn't *know* what Deuce meant…but couldn't they wonder about it a little? Make a few guesses? Anything would be better than spending hours in the too-quiet Libury, flipping through boring books that had basically nothing to do with Deuce and his mysterious message.

Cleo scanned one of the books. "This says that in addition to mainland Greece, there are hundreds of Greek islands."

Draculaura looked up. "I didn't know that," she replied. Then she returned to the paragraph she'd been reading.

"They're located in the Aegean Sea," Cleo said.

"Cool," Draculaura said. She didn't look up this time.

"They have a lot of mountains," Cleo added.

"Um, you know what?" Draculaura said, clearly choosing her words carefully. "I bet this will go even faster if we do all our research first, then share our facts all at once—with Frankie and Clawdeen. What do you think?"

"Oh. Sure. Of course," Cleo agreed quickly. "Great idea, Drac!"

Cleo flipped the page. She tried to concentrate, she really did, but all the words seemed to swim back and forth on the page. She forgot every sentence almost as quickly as she read it. Cleo didn't even realize when she sighed again, louder this time.

Draculaura glanced up from her book. "Everything okay?" she asked.

"Sorry," Cleo apologized. "I can't concentrate. It's like the minute I read something, I forget it.

Maybe I should take notes or something. But I left my notebook downstairs in the lab—*ugh!* My brain is so fried!"

Draculaura smiled sympathetically. "I know what you mean. We already got a brain workout in the lab this morning," she replied.

"Exactly!" Cleo exclaimed.

"Tell you what," Draculaura said. "Why don't you take a walk? You could 'clear the cobwebs from your head,' like my dad always says." She paused and made a face. "Ugh, did I really just quote my *dad?*"

Cleo giggled. "Don't worry—I won't tell anyone," she replied. "But I don't want to leave you here with all this work."

"No worries," Draculaura assured her. "I think this book has just about everything we need in it. So hopefully our research is going to take less time than we thought."

"Golden!" Cleo exclaimed. "Thanks, Draculaura—I really owe you one!"

ॐ   ॐ   ॐ

As Cleo left the Libury, her first thought was to go straight to her dorm room and pick out the perfect outfit for their rescue mission. But she caught a glance of the ghoulgeous weather outside and decided to take Draculaura's advice. *Maybe a walk around campus really will clear my head*, she thought.

As she roamed the grounds, Cleo could hear tons of activity from the other students. Some of her fellow members of the fearleading squad were hard at work on their pyramid formations. Cleo smiled as she watched them, remembering all the pyramids back home in Egypt—including the one where she'd been trapped for hundreds of years, thanks to a beeswax candle mishap. Cleo remembered how eager she'd been for Draulaura,

Clawdeen, and Frankie to rescue her. *That's probably why I'm so excited to get started on our mission to rescue Deuce*, she told herself. *I know exactly how he feels. That's one thing that Deuce and I have in common, at least!*

And the sun! It was beating down with a ferocity that was all too familiar to Cleo from her days in the desert. *I bet Lagoona was right*, she thought as her mind wandered back to Deuce's video. *He was probably just shielding his eyes from the sun... not, like, hiding some horrible secret or something.*

Even here, in the courtyard at Monster High, the sun was a powerful force. Cleo was big on jewelry—in fact, no one at Monster High had ever seen her without her signature chandelier earrings or gold collar necklace. But on a day so intensely bright, Cleo's bling was a definite distraction. It winked and flashed whenever she moved. Normally, Cleo loved the way her jewelry flashed light onto her face, like a personal spotlight that highlighted her every move. But today, as it blazed right in her eyes, she found herself squinting against the brightness.

I really need some shades, she thought, shielding her eyes just as Deuce had in the video.

And that's when Cleo had her idea—her totally golden idea! If it was so bright in Greece that Deuce couldn't even make a superfast video without having to protect his eyes, then Cleo and her ghoulfriends would *definitely* need some eye protection for their rescue mission. And there was absolutely no reason why it shouldn't be fabulous and fashionable too.

I'll design it myself, Cleo thought excitedly. *A custom pair for each one of us! We will look totally ghoulgeous!*

Then Cleo had an even more thrilling thought. *And I can make a pair of shades for Deuce too!* she thought. *He'll be so surprised—and I bet he'll be really touched at how thoughtful I am—I mean, we are.*

Cleo climbed the stairs two at a time until she

reached the art room. Clawdeen's mom, the art teacher at Monster High, kept the large, airy studio space open twenty-four hours a day in case any of her students felt a sudden burst of creativity. Cleo grabbed a handful of metallic colored pencils and a sketchbook and went right to work.

I might not be able to remember the difference between refraction and reflection, she thought, *but I know when reflective sunglasses are an absolute necessity!*

After Cleo sketched a pair of sunglasses for Deuce—bold red flames and dark lenses with a silvery mirrored coating—she sat back and stared at her work. *Not bad, for someone who doesn't exactly have a ton of design experience,* she thought. *But I think I'd better get a little help before I design the rest of them.*

And Cleo knew just who to ask: Clawdeen! Clawdeen's artistic side was legendary, and she would *definitely* know how to advise Cleo on sunglasses design.

Cleo carefully tore her sketch out of the sketchbook and made her way toward the Howl of History in search of Clawdeen. To her surprise, the Howl of History was empty. *Is it already time to meet up at the Creepeteria?* she wondered.

Sure enough, when Cleo arrived at the Creepeteria, she found Draculaura waiting for her.

"There you are!" Draculaura cried. "Did you forget the meeting time?"

"Yikes—am I that late?" Cleo asked, glancing around. "Frankie and Clawdeen aren't even here yet."

"They were here already and are now gone to get supplies for our mission," Draculaura corrected her. "When they get back, we'll be ready to leave!"

Cleo's mouth dropped open. "Seriously? So soon?" she shrieked.

"Yeah, you'll never believe what Clawdeen and Frankie learned about ancient Greek monsters," Draculaura said, lowering her voice so no one would overhear her. "I mean, we're talking some of the creepiest, craziest beasties you can imagine!"

Cleo smiled knowingly. "Remember, I've got some experience with curses, hexes, and mummies with a temper," she joked.

"That's the best news I've heard all day," Draculaura replied. She held up the book she'd been reading so Cleo could read the title: *Most Menacing Monsters*. "Frankie brought this from the Howl of History. Sure, there are incredible flying creatures like Pegasus and the gold-loving griffins, but just reading about these monsters is going to give me nightmares for *weeks*."

"So listen—before we get going, I had an idea," Cleo began. She pulled out her sunglasses sketch, but before she could tell Draculaura all about her big plan, Clawdeen and Frankie hurried up to their table.

"Ready—set—go!" Frankie announced as she dropped the ghouls' fully loaded backpacks on the table.

"We've got it all," Clawdeen added. "Scuba gear? Check. Boo-noculars? Check."

"And I whipped up a new batch of sunscream," Frankie said.

"Everything we need for a mission to the Greek isles!" Draculaura announced.

"Why the scuba suits?" Cleo asked curiously. They'd come in really handy for rescuing Lagoona from the Great Barrier Reef, but in his video, Deuce had clearly been standing on dry land.

"Just to be on the safe side," Frankie explained. "Greece is made up of thousands of islands! So we're hoping that the Monster Mapalogue will leave us on dry land..."

"But you never know," Draculaura said with a laugh. There had been plenty of islands in the

43

Great Barrier Reef too, but the Monster Mapalogue had dropped them right in the middle of the ocean!

"Do you think we should change into our scuba suits before we leave?" Clawdeen asked, glancing at Frankie. Everyone knew that an accidental dip in salt water could make her short-circuit—or even corrode her bolts.

I hope not, Cleo thought anxiously. The scuba suits that Frankie had designed were really useful…but not exactly what she wanted to wear when she met any new monsters for the very first time.

"I should change—just to be on the safe side," Frankie said. "But the rest of you ghouls can probably take a chance."

Cleo breathed a sigh of relief as Frankie hurried off to change into her scuba suit. Draculaura misunderstood and gave her arm a sympathetic squeeze.

"I hope you're not worried about the water, Cleo," she said. "You've come really far with your swimming skills! And we can grab a life vest if it would make you feel better."

"No, that's not it," Cleo replied. "It's just—I had an idea about something we'll need for this rescue mission too!"

She unfolded her sketch and placed it in the center of the table. "Ta-da!"

"Oooh! Sunglasses?" Clawdeen asked. "They look clawesome!"

Cleo beamed. "Thank you! I thought we could each have a custom pair. Check out the reflective lenses—not bad, huh? I mean, honestly, they do double duty. Shield your eyes and check your makeup!"

"Love it," Draculaura announced. "I want some!"

"That's exactly what I had in mind," Cleo said. "I thought we could make some—a pair for each of us. It can't be that hard, right?"

Clawdeen took a closer look at the sketch. "The design looks good to me," Clawdeen said. "But I'm not sure how to make sunglasses."

"We'd need a mold, to start," Frankie said thoughtfully as she rejoined the group. "We can mix up different polymers for the frame...a custom one for each pair, I suppose, to get the colors right, and to customize them with any add-ins like glitter."

Cleo frowned just a little. "That sounds like it would take a long time," she said.

"Not as long as it will take to make the lenses," Frankie replied. "They'll need to be cut and polished, of course...give the reflective coating time to set...and then the fitting, to make sure each pair fits just right..."

"*Hmm,*" Draculaura said. "Making five pairs of custom sunglasses sounds like a pretty big project."

"They'd be nice to have—but I'm not sure they're absolutely necessary," Clawdeen added.

"I guess you're right," Cleo said, sounding a little disappointed. "It wouldn't be fair to make Deuce wait any longer. He's waiting for us, like, *now.*"

"It *is* a great idea, though," Draculaura told Cleo. "Maybe we can make them when we get back!"

"Yeah! I love mixing up polymer composites," Frankie said brightly.

"I don't even know what that means, but it sounds good to me," Cleo said, smiling again. She folded her sketch and tucked it into her pocket. "Okay, ghouls—what are we waiting for? Greece awaits!"

"Wait—we can't leave from here," Draculaura said, glancing around. "Too many monsters."

"Let's go to the Libury, then," Cleo said impatiently. "It was deserted, remember?"

Once the ghouls were alone in the Libury, Draculaura held out the Skullette; her hands were steady, but her heart was pounding. There was no way to know what excitement, adventure—and even danger—were in store.

After the other ghouls placed their fingers on the Skullette, Draculaura took a deep breath and said the special incantation: *"Deuce. Exsto monstrum!"*

Whooosh!

CHAPTER 5

Draculaura's head was spinning—she couldn't tell if her eyes were open or not—she couldn't *see* anything—but she could feel. And what she felt was millions of grains of sand shifting beneath her fingers.

It took a moment for her to register how hot they were. But when Draculaura realized, she jumped to her feet as fast as she could so no part of her skin was touching the blazing sand.

"Ghouls?" she said, unsure. *Why* couldn't she see? It wasn't dark—no, that wasn't the problem—

It was *bright.*

Too bright.

Draculaura remembered Deuce's video and cupped her hand over her eyes. Slowly, they started to adjust to the brightness, and she realized that she was standing on a wide white beach. The dazzling ocean, just a few feet away, only added to the brightness as it reflected the glittering sun.

"Drac!"

Cleo's voice was faint, carried away by the ocean breeze. But it was enough for Draculaura to know she was near.

"Frankie! Clawdeen!" Draculaura called.

Slowly, her ghoulfriends came into focus. They took tentative steps as if they too were having trouble seeing.

"Let's get over to the shade," Draculaura said. "Come on!"

The four ghouls linked arms and took careful steps toward a shaded area, where the white-hot sand transformed, becoming cool and silvery.

"Wow," Draculaura said. "We made it! I think! This looks just like the pictures in the libury books. That sand! That sea!"

"That was a close call, huh?" Frankie asked, tugging at the neck of her scuba suit. "We nearly landed in the ocean!"

"I think that's the Aegean Sea," Draculaura said, remembering Cleo's research.

"I bet Lagoona will be sorry she missed this mission!" Clawdeen cracked.

"Why are we here?" Cleo said. "As much as I'd love a beach day to keep my golden skin just perfectly golden, it didn't exactly look like Deuce was on the beach in his video. Do you think the Monster Mapalogue messed up?"

"I don't know..." Draculaura said slowly. "It's never let us down before. I mean, even when it dropped us in the middle of the ocean, that was just because Lagoona was especially close by."

Cleo squinted up at the sky.

"Careful," Frankie warned her. "Don't stare straight at the sun."

"I won't," Cleo promised. "I thought there was a cloud bank up there...but I think it's a building."

"I think you're right!" Draculaura exclaimed. "It's all white....I think I see columns..."

"Deuce was leaning against a column in his video!" Cleo cried. "I remember that!"

"Wow," Clawdeen said, looking at her closely. "You have a good memory, Cleo."

Cleo smiled and fanned her face, which felt really warm all of a sudden. "Thanks," she said. "Would you pass me some of that sunscream?"

"Sure—and I'm going to ditch my scuba suit, since we're on dry land," Frankie replied. "It's *hot!*"

"I bet you anything that's one of the ancient outdoor amphitheaters," Draculaura said, her voice high with excitement. "They were used for sports...plays...all kinds of entertainment."

"And you think Deuce is just, like, fanging out up there?" asked Cleo.

"Why not?" Draculaura replied. "You're the one who recognized the columns."

"Then what are we waiting for?" Cleo asked. "Let's go!"

"There's just one question," Frankie spoke up. "*How* are we going to get up there? Climb the cliff?"

"I suppose it's too much to hope for an escalator," Clawdeen added.

The ghouls were all silent for a moment, trying to figure out the easiest—and most efficient—way to reach the coliseum at the top of that tall cliff. That's when Draculaura suddenly heard something...odd.

It wasn't the soothing sounds of the ocean waves or the whisper of the breeze whipping over the water.

No. It was almost a...panting sound.

Despite the warmth, Draculaura shivered.

"Ghouls," she whispered. "Do you...hear that?"

Everyone paused to listen. Draculaura could tell from the shifting expressions on her ghoulfriends' faces that, yes, once she pointed out the strange sound, they could hear it too.

For a long moment, no one spoke.

Then a look of recognition flitted across Clawdeen's face—for just a moment. "It almost... it almost sounds like my little brothers when they're sleeping," she said. "But...that can't be possible...can it?"

Can it? Draculaura thought, panic creeping over her. *Can the Monster Mapalogue transport others too? If they're, like, nearby when it's in use?* Clawdeen's little brothers lived at Monster High too, just like her mom, though they were still too young to take classes. What if they'd snuck up on Clawdeen— they loved to tackle her and roughhouse when she least expected it—just as Draculaura said the magic words, and the Monster Mapalogue whisked them to the other side of the world too? But that would be ridiculous...right?

Draculaura hoped more than anything that Clawdeen was wrong. How in the world would they tackle a rescue mission with a bunch of little werepups tackling *them*? She was sure this was the worst thing that could've happened.

Draculaura glanced around, expecting to see a rough-and-tumble jumble of werewolf cubs—but what her eyes spotted was worse.

Way, way worse.

Draculaura's mouth went dry. She had to swallow hard, twice, before she could speak.

"Ghouls," she began, "don't look now—but I think we found our first monster!"

CHAPTER 6

Where?" Cleo squealed, looking around expectantly. "Is it Deuce?"

"*Shhhh!*" Draculaura whispered, clamping her hand over Cleo's mouth. Cleo's eyes widened with outrage—until she saw the terror in Draculaura's face. "Don't make a sound!"

"You're freaking us out, Drac," Frankie said in a low voice. "What's wrong?"

"Over there," Draculaura replied with a small

jerk of her head. "I think...no...I *know*...that's Cerberus."

All the ghouls turned to look into the distance and saw a strange looking hill or mountain that was dark and maybe a bit...fuzzy?

"Is that the name of that mountain?" Clawdeen asked doubtfully.

"That's not a mountain!" Draculaura said. "It's a beastie! See how it's moving, ever so slowly, up and down, up and down—because it's *breathing? And how it's so big we can feel its breath from here?*"

"Who or what is a Cerberus?" asked Cleo haughtily. "And why does it sound like he or she or it is about to get in the way of this rescue mission! Not that...you know...I'm in a hurry to meet Deuce or anything. I'm not. It's just, you know... I have a busy schedule and—*what?*" The ghouls stared at Cleo, then burst out in laughter. They'd never seen her act so *uncool* before! Cleo blushed.

"Moving on.... You were saying, Drac? About the big, hairy monster breathing in the distance?"

"Oh, right, that's just the ferocious guard dog to the underworld, or so they say," Draculaura explained with an awkward laugh. "His whole purpose in life is just to... well, keep dead people from escaping."

"*Ewww!*" Cleo said, wrinkling her nose.

Frankie looked confused. "Draculaura?" she began. "I think he's sick or something. His breathing is really weird—all different speeds."

Draculaura gulped. "That's probably because he has three separate heads with three sets of razor-sharp teeth," she said. "Did I forget to mention that?"

"Bet you anything that guard dog is guarding the way up," Frankie said, looking more interested by the minute. "I wish we could get closer. I'd love to study a three-headed beastie."

"Ugh. No, thank you," Cleo complained. "Well, let's just sneak past him."

"I don't think it's going to be that easy," Draculaura replied. "Don't you think the whole *point* of Cerberus being here is to guard the cliff—and whatever's up there?"

"I don't know," Clawdeen said. "Maybe he just felt like a day at the beach. I know I could use a roll in the white sand."

Draculaura rummaged around in her backpack until she found the boo-noculars. She stared through them and exclaimed, "Ghouls! Cerberus is guarding something—a set of stairs carved into the mountainside!"

"If whatever's up there is so dangerous it needs a guard…maybe we should rethink our plan of climbing to the top," Frankie pointed out.

"Let's vote," Cleo said impatiently. "Everyone in favor of sneaking past that stinky-breath mutt and climbing to the top of the cliff now, raise your hand."

Cleo's and Clawdeen's hands shot into the air. Cleo gave Draculaura and Frankie a pointed look, but they didn't budge.

"Okay," Cleo said, annoyed. "Everyone who thinks we should just fang out here and waste more time, raise your hand."

"Come on, Cleo," Draculaura said. "How about, 'Everyone who thinks we should make sure we have thought through our options before we rush off and mess with one of the worst monsters in Greek history, or sneak up some heavily guarded stairs that lead who knows where, raise your hand?'"

Draculaura raised her hand. Frankie did too— for a moment. Then it fell off her arm and flopped into the sand!

"Whoops," she said. "My bad!"

"Well, that's a bit wordy for my taste, but suit yourself. So that's two votes for climbing the cliff, one vote for doing nothing, and one abstention," Cleo announced. "Let's go!"

"No way!" Draculaura argued. "Frankie's hand fell off! She didn't even get a chance to cast her vote!"

"Ghouls," Clawdeen said.

"I mean, I *did* cast my vote; it's just my hand fell off," Frankie pointed out.

"Uh, *ghouls*," Clawdeen said again.

"Please, ghouls!" Cleo argued. "Besides, don't you think the Monster Mapalogue left us here for a reason? Because this is the closest, easiest way to get to Deuce?"

"Ghouls!" Clawdeen exclaimed, so loudly that everyone turned to her.

"*Shh!*" Draculaura said, placing at finger to her lips. "You'll wake Cerberus!"

"It's too late," Clawdeen replied grimly. "You already did!"

Draculaura spun around in horror. Sure enough,

the massive, monstrous beast had pulled himself up to his full height. Six bloodshot eyes narrowed as they focused on the ghouls; on all three heads, Cerberus's lips curled back in a snarl, revealing row after row of glistening, drooly fangs.

A low, rumbling growl—actually, *three* growls—ricocheted across the sands, nearly knocking the ghouls backward.

Draculaura and her ghoulfriends screamed!

But not just terror—also disgust. Cleo clamped her nose shut and said, "*Ewww*, did you smell his breath?" she complained. "Seriously stinky! I knew there was a reason I've always loved cats best."

This time, Cerberus's growl sounded more like a roar!

Cleo grimaced, waving her hand in front of her face. "If he does that again, I'm going to need, like, *ten* baths before I can meet Deuce—" Cleo froze, realizing what she'd said. "I mean…before I can meet anyone. A princess must look her absolutely best at all times...right? Ha. Ha."

Clawdeen was about to comment on Cleo's slipup when suddenly, the ground started to shake. It wasn't an earthquake, though. Cerberus was charging right at them!

"Ghoul, smelling bad is the *least* of our worries," Draculaura said. "We've got to move—*now!*"

She grabbed Cleo's arm and raced across the sand, with Clawdeen and Frankie right behind them. Draculaura's fingers rested on the Skullette around her neck. If they had to—if they absolutely *had* to escape—

"You're not going to use that, are you?" Cleo called out, as if she could read Draculaura's mind. "We just got here!"

"We're not going to last very long if we can't find a hiding place from Cerberus!" Draculaura shot back. "I mean, did you *see* those *teeth?*"

"*Fangs* would be the more accurate term,"

 63

Frankie spoke up. "And Draculaura's right. At the rate Cerberus is running, he's covering ground a *lot* faster than we are."

"Any ideas, Clawdeen?" Draculaura called back to Clawdeen. "Aren't you, like, an expert in taming wild pups? What do you do when you babysit your brothers?"

"I can't think of anything—unless you ghouls thought to pack dog treats!" Clawdeen replied.

"Dog treats definitely did *not* make the list," noted Frankie.

But mentioning dog treats—and thinking of her brothers—gave Clawdeen another idea. She glanced around until she spotted a piece of driftwood poking out of the sand. Then she lunged over, yanked it out, and yelled, "Hey, Cerberus—fetch!"

With all her might, Clawdeen tossed the stick away from the ghouls. It sailed through the air—but Cerberus didn't even seem to notice it.

"Sorry, ghouls," Clawdeen said. "That was my best idea—and it was a total flop."

"No—it was a *great* idea," Frankie exclaimed. "There was just one problem, though—the stick was too small!"

"Huh?" asked Draculaura.

"For a game of fetch, a giant monster-dog needs a giant stick," Frankie explained. "We'd probably have to throw, like, an entire tree trunk for Cerberus to notice it."

"Good point," Clawdeen said. "There's just one problem. We're in the middle of a beach—not the middle of the forest."

"And trees don't really grow on beaches," added Cleo.

"Ghouls, use your imaginations," Frankie urged them. She rummaged around in her backpack and pulled out a coil of rope. "If the sticks we've got aren't big enough, we'll just have to make our own."

"Like a Frankenstick," Clawdeen joked.

"Exactly!" Frankie replied. "Everybody grab a handful of driftwood, and I'll try to figure some kind of device that will help us throw the bunch as far as we possibly can."

"Do we have time for that?" Cleo asked anxiously, glancing back at Cerberus.

"I don't think we have a choice," Draculaura replied. "Let's go!"

Draculaura, Cleo, and Clawdeen gathered armfuls of the smooth, gnarled driftwood as quickly as they could. They wrapped all the pieces of driftwood together, securing them with the thick rope.

"Ugh!" Draculaura groaned as she tried to lift the Frankenstick. "This is definitely big enough for Cerberus to see—but how are we going to lift it? It weighs a ton!"

"No worries!" Frankie spoke up. She held up her hands and announced, "Ta-da!"

"Wow!" Cleo said, squinting up at Frankie's creation. "Uh...what is it, exactly?"

"A combination slingshot-catapult," Frankie said proudly. "This stretchy rope has a special compartment for the Frankenstick. Those two poles provide support. Pull back on the rope and *fwing!* It should launch the Frankenstick to the stratosphere! Okay, maybe that's a *tiny* exaggeration—"

Cleo didn't let her finish. "Golden idea, Frankie! I love it!" she cheered.

Frankie grinned. "I had a feeling that we were going to need a little help launching the stick," she replied. "After all, we don't just need to throw the Frankenstick—we need to throw it really, *really* far to get him away from us."

"Whoa!" Draculaura said suddenly as the ground shook. "Earthquake?"

"Nope," Clawdeen said, shaking her head. "Cerberus is getting closer!"

"There's no time to lose," Frankie said. "Cleo, Clawdeen—you hold the sides steady. Draculaura, you position the stick in the launch receptacle. And I'll handle the launch."

The other ghouls understood perfectly. There was a flurry of activity as they rushed into position.

"Is this right?" Draculaura asked, sounding worried. "I've never put a driftwood Frankenstick into a catapult-thingy."

"It's great," Frankie assured her. "Now—step aside, Drac!—on the count of three..."

"One," Cleo said.

"Two," Clawdeen said.

"Three!" the ghouls cried, all at the same time.

Frankie took a deep breath and sliced through the cord. Draculaura held her breath—she almost couldn't bear to watch, but she couldn't look away, either. This plan was their *only* chance to distract Cerberus...and Draculaura didn't know what they'd do if it failed.

Shhhhhhhhwwwwwwwwweeeeeeeeeeeeeeeeeeee!

A high-pitched whistling sound filled the air as Frankie's catapult launched the stick at top speed! It was so loud and shrill that Cerberus, with his six supersensitive ears, skidded to a stop.

Oh no, Draculaura thought. *What if that sound is hurting his ears—and he gets more upset with us?*

The Frankenstick turned end over end as it arced through the sky, flying so high and so far that in seconds it was almost impossible to see.

Not for Cerberus, though!

With a loud, bone-shaking bark, the enormous beast began to gallop across the sand—in the opposite direction from the ghouls! Clawdeen and Frankie's plan had succeeded beyond their wildest dreams! The ghouls shrieked with glee, high-fiving one another as they celebrated.

Even the trembling vibrations of the ground lessened as Cerberus galloped farther and farther away.

"At last, our rescue mission is back on track!" Cleo declared. "Now, where were we?"

"We were just about to—" Draculaura began. Suddenly, she stopped speaking.

"Go on," Clawdeen prompted her.

"Did you—feel that?" Draculaura whispered. "I think the ground is shaking again."

"I didn't feel anything," Cleo said. "You probably still *remember* the ground shaking. Or maybe your legs are wobbly. I mean, that was *really* scary and all."

"Maybe," Draculaura said doubtfully. "I just—"

"I feel it too," Frankie said suddenly. "And my legs are definitely not wobbly."

"Me too," added Clawdeen.

Without saying another word, all four ghouls

turned toward the direction in which Cerberus had disappeared. It didn't take long for their worst fears to be realized.

Cerberus was charging at them—with the Frankenstick clamped in one of his mouths!

CHAPTER 7

"What are we going to do now?" Cleo cried.

"We don't have time to make a new Frankenstick," Frankie said. "If my calculations are correct, at the pace Cerberus is traveling, he'll be here in—"

"Like, *right now!*" Clawdeen yelled. "We've got to run!"

"Run *where?*" Cleo asked. "Unless Frankie's got some kind of jet pack or antigravity device in her backpack, we'll never be able to escape in time!"

"I don't—but those are great ideas for our next rescue mission," Frankie said.

"What next rescue mission?" Cleo snapped. "We're about to be eaten by a mythological monster from ancient Greece!"

"Maybe not!" Draculaura replied frantically. "Maybe there's another option—another plan—something—*anything*—"

But even as she said the words, Cerberus was bounding across the sand. His speed seemed to increase the closer he got, until by the time the last word escaped from Draculaura's mouth, he was looming over them, blocking even the bright sun with his shaggy black fur.

The ghouls grabbed one another's hands and screamed! Draculaura squeezed her eyes shut tight. At least she wasn't alone. At least her best ghoulfriends were by her side, no matter what happened next—even if Cerberus chewed them into bits or carted them off to the underworld—

Or licked them with three scratchy, slobbery puppy tongues—

Draculaura cringed, waiting for something even worse to happen. Instead, she heard a happy panting noise. She opened one eye—and saw Cerberus sitting on his haunches, all three tongues lolling out of his mouths! He panted happily and nudged the Frankenstick, which he'd dropped at the ghouls' feet, closer toward them.

"Is it over?" Clawdeen asked, her eyes still tightly shut. "Are we in Cerberus's belly yet?"

"No," Draculaura said, giggling. "Open your eyes, ghouls. Cerberus doesn't want to eat us—he wants to play!"

Cleo's eyes fluttered open, then immediately narrowed. "Hold up. You're telling me that one of the most fearsome monsters of ancient Greece wants to *play* with us?"

"Looks that way," Clawdeen said as Cerberus

rolled over on his back with his paws up in the air. "Who wants his tummy rubbed? Who? Who? Is it you? Is it Cerberus?"

"Give me a break," Cleo grumbled. But when one of Cerberus's heads nuzzled her shiny gold sandal, even Cleo couldn't resist scratching behind his ears.

"Ooh, he likes that," Clawdeen said as Cerberus's thick tail went *thump-thump-thump*, kicking up a dusty cloud of sand.

"I bet Cerberus would love to play a few rounds of fetch," Draculaura said. "Should we fire up Frankie's catapult?"

"We can't spend all day playing, though," Cleo said, glancing toward the sun. "Before we know it, the sun will start setting."

"You want to tell Cerberus that belly-rub time is over?" Clawdeen asked. "Be my guest."

Cleo made a face at her. Sure, Cerberus was

acting like a big, lovable puppy *now*. But none of the ghouls wanted to find out what he'd do if he stopped getting his way.

"Cleo has a point," Draculaura said. "We *are* here on a rescue mission." She turned to Frankie and Clawdeen. "What else do you remember from your research?" she asked. "Were there any other facts about Cerberus that could help?"

Frankie ticked them off on her fingers. "Three heads, rumored guard of the underworld, said to be the personal pet pooch of Hades himself, ferocious *and* terrifying..."

"There was one myth," Draculaura said thoughtfully, "where somebody put Cerberus to sleep by singing him a lullaby."

"You're kidding," Clawdeen replied. "A lullaby?"

"I'll try anything if it gets our mission back on track," Cleo said. She opened her mouth and started to sing. To everyone's surprise, Cerberus's eyelids began to droop.

"Cleo! You did it!" Draculaura whispered.

"*Shhh!*" Cleo replied. The girls moved away from the sleeping Cerberus so they could come up with a plan.

"Now what are we going to do?" asked Frankie.

As the sun started to descend, it looked more orange than gold. Draculaura didn't know exactly how much time they had before night fell, but she had a feeling it wasn't enough.

"Well," she began, "we still want to get to the top of the mount, right? Where we saw the pillars?"

"You know it, ghoul," Cleo replied. "I'm *sure* Deuce is up there. No doubt."

"But we can't climb up here," Draculaura continued, gesturing to the steep stone wall behind them. "It's too smooth. I can't even see any footholds."

"So let's just go back to where we first saw Cerberus and that staircase he was guarding," Cleo said, flicking some sand off her shoulder. "Problem solved."

"Not exactly," Frankie spoke up.

Everyone turned to look at her.

"I think we're on the opposite end of the island," she said. "I know we weren't exactly paying attention while we tried to escape from Cerberus, but it appears that we traveled farther than we realized."

"So what are you saying, exactly?" Clawdeen asked.

"I'm saying that it will probably take us a few *hours* to get back to where we started," Frankie said. "Unless you're all in the mood for another wild run over the sand?"

"Seriously?" Cleo groaned. "I'm exhausted!"

"Me too," Draculaura admitted. "And even if we ran the whole way, I'm not sure we could make it before the sun sets."

"Yeah," Frankie agreed. "I think you're right."

For a long moment, no one spoke.

"Oh!" Draculaura suddenly exclaimed. "The Monster Mapalogue!"

"What about it?" asked Clawdeen.

"Maybe it will take us back to where it left us before," Draculaura said, her voice high with excitement. "Come on, ghouls!"

Everyone put their fingers on the Skullette as Draculaura chanted, *"Deuce. Exsto monstrum!"*

The ghouls waited expectantly…but nothing happened.

"Why isn't it working?" Draculaura asked.

A half smile flickered across Frankie's face. "Because we're already so close to Deuce," she guessed. "He's at the top of this mountain—we're just on the wrong side of it, and we'll have to walk all the way around to get to the stairs. As far as the Monster Mapalogue knows, we're *there* already."

"Just not close enough to get to him before

nightfall," Draculaura said. She couldn't hide the disappointment in her voice.

"So…are we giving up?" asked Cleo.

"No way!" Draculaura said firmly. "Nobody said *anything* about giving up!"

"But we're not equipped for an overnight," Frankie said. "Even though camping out on the beach sounds pretty sparktacular."

Cleo glanced off to the side, her face creased with disappointment. The other ghouls were surprised. She seemed to be taking the setback hard—really hard. And that wasn't like her.

"Hey," Clawdeen said. "We'll come back first thing tomorrow morning. It's not the end of the world. You heard Drac. We are *not* giving up. You know that's not our style."

"I know," Cleo said quietly. "I mean…it's not like this mission is special or anything. It's just that we're basically monster rescue specialists, and I just can't believe that there isn't *some* way for us to—"

Suddenly, Cleo gasped.

"What? What is it?" Draculaura asked. She glanced around urgently. "Another monster?"

"No—I mean, yes—I mean, I hope so!" Cleo cried. She turned to Draculaura. "That book—what you were telling me—the Creepeteria—the—with the wings—do you remember? Do *you?*"

The other ghouls stared at her blankly.

"Ghoul, I hate to break it to you, but you're not exactly making sense," Clawdeen said. "Try adding a few more nouns."

Cleo took a slow, deep breath and tried to calm herself down. "There were these monsters Draculaura told me about," she said slowly, emphasizing every word. "With massive wings. You know. Flying mythological creatures?"

"The griffins!" Frankie exclaimed.

"Yes!" Cleo was practically shouting. "Griffins!"

"With lion bodies and eagle wings, griffins are among the most majestic and powerful of all creatures," Frankie said.

"*And* they fly!" Cleo added. "So all we need to do is get a pack of griffins over here and have them *fly* us up to the top of the mount!"

"Cleo! You're a genius!" Draculaura exclaimed. Then a new thought struck her. "But, uh, *how* exactly will we attract a pack of griffins?"

Cleo's eyes twinkled. "Easy," she declared, holding out her arm and shaking it so her bangle bracelets slid back and forth. "Didn't you say that griffins love gold?"

"Yes!" Clawdeen said. "That's right. Griffins love bling."

"Well, obviously, they have great taste, and we're going to get along just fine," Cleo announced. She strode across the sand and stepped into a patch of blazing sunlight.

"Griffins!" she called out, shaking her arms so her bracelets clinked and clanked.

The other ghouls stared at the sky.

"Griffins!" Cleo called, louder this time. She waved her arms over her head, making her bracelets sparkle and shine. "Griffins! Where are you?"

CHAPTER 8

As the minutes ticked away, Draculaura, Frankie, and Clawdeen exchanged a worried glance. Cleo hadn't given up—her arms were still high in the sky, her bracelets still glittering—but there was no sign of griffins, and it was getting later and later.

"Maybe we *should* try something different," Clawdeen finally said. "It's been a long time…"

Cleo shook her head. "Not yet," she replied.

"Let's just give it a few more minutes," said Frankie sympathetically.

"But I really think—" Clawdeen began.

Cleo shook her head again, harder this time. Her brilliant gold earrings flashed as they swung back and forth.

Thwak-thwak-thwak-thwak.

It came from overhead, a thunderous noise that demanded everyone's attention. Draculaura shielded her eyes as she glanced up at the sky. There was a dark spot in the distance, silhouetted against the setting sun, but as Draculaura watched, it got bigger and bigger as it came closer and closer. The noise grew louder, and suddenly Draculaura could feel a breeze fluttering her long pink-streaked hair.

Wings, she realized, her heart fluttering excitedly. It could only be massive wings flapping as the griffins soared through the sky.

"Cleo!" Draculaura cried out. "You did it! You called the griffins!"

"I know, ghoul!" Cleo called back. "But keep your voice down, please. Don't startle them."

The ghouls watched in awed silence as a dozen stunning griffins swooped down to the sand, coming to a perfect landing several feet away. If Draculaura hadn't been so awed by the griffins, she would've been terrified: Their lion bodies were enormous, with powerful muscles rippling under their gleaming golden fur. Even their feathers seemed to shine, iridescent rainbows that glimmered in the sunlight. It was a breathtaking sight to behold.

Draculaura wasn't sure what to do next. She glanced over at Cleo uncertainly, only to see that Cleo had a beaming smile on her face. "Now, *that's* my kind of mythical creature," Cleo whispered.

With a toss of her head—swishing her long hair over her shoulder and sending her earrings shimmying lightly again—Cleo strode confidently toward the griffins. "I'm so glad you're here," she began. "If you'd just—"

An earsplitting cry stopped Cleo in her tracks. Part roar, part shriek, it was unmistakable: a warning. Cleo paused before taking another cautious step forward.

"Cleo! Stop!" Clawdeen hissed. "Don't get any closer!"

"Yeah!" added Frankie. "Do I have to remind you that's a bird of prey crossed with one of the world's deadliest mammals?"

"I'm not afraid," Cleo said. "This griffin and I have a lot in common. Don't we, you beautiful beast, you?"

And with that, Cleo shook out her arm again. Her bracelets rang like musical chimes.

Cleo took another step forward. This time, the griffin didn't make a sound…but it did turn its head curiously.

Cleo flashed a triumphant smile at her ghoul-friends. "What did I tell you?" she said.

"Be careful," Clawdeen warned her. "You have no idea what it's going to do next!"

As if on cue, the griffin opened its beak and cried out again. Its long, glittering talon shot forward and drew a line in the sand. The message was clear: *Don't come any closer.*

Cleo froze. She stood in the sand, staring at the griffin, lost in thought.

"We've got to get her out of there!" Clawdeen hissed.

"Let's just wait another minute," Frankie said. "She was right about the griffins... and right about how to attract them."

Cleo held out her arm again. Then, in one long, swift motion, she swept every single bracelet off her arm!

Draculaura, Frankie, and Clawdeen gasped in shock. Cleo, however, didn't miss a beat. With the bracelets in a precarious stack in her outstretched hand, she took another tentative step toward the griffin. Then another...and another...

"Do you like them?" Cleo asked the majestic creature. "Absolutely golden, aren't they? They're made from the finest gold and gems in all Egypt. They've been in the royal family for centuries. Millennia! Of course, I'm sure you can appreciate their regal lineage. King of birds and king of beasts combined...you certainly look like you deserve the best, only the best, and nothing but..."

With every word, Cleo took another step closer...and closer...and closer! From her outstretched hand, it looked as if she were offering her bracelets to the griffin. As if she were going to just give them away. But that couldn't be right, Draculaura knew. Cleo loved her jewelry more than, well, just about anything...especially the exquisite royal pieces that marked her as a princess.

Suddenly, Cleo was just inches away from the griffin. Draculaura had no idea what she would do next—and for a second, she wondered if even Cleo knew! Then, to her surprise, Cleo knelt down on the sand and held up her bracelets, as if she were offering them to the griffin.

Wait, Draculaura suddenly realized. *She is offering it her bracelets.*

Then, to everyone's astonishment, the griffin lowered its head to Cleo's hand. It nudged her hand, making the bangles fall to the ground. Then the griffin looped them over its talons, like rings!

Cleo glanced over her shoulder and grinned at her ghoulfriends. "See? Now it's my beastie bestie," she joked. Then she turned back to the griffin and said, "So, listen, can I ask you a really big favor? My ghouls and I are trying to get to the top of the mount before dark. Is there any way you could give us a ride?"

The griffin stared at her for a long moment.

Did it even understand what Cleo had asked? Draculaura couldn't tell.

The griffin made a strange sound to the rest of the pack, a series of cries and clicks with its beak. Draculaura had never heard anything like it.

Three griffins came forward to join the one wearing Cleo's bangles. Then all four griffins knelt down. The message was clear: They were inviting the ghouls to climb onto their backs!

"Come on, ghouls!" Cleo cried. "We're going to ride in style!"

Draculaura, Frankie, and Clawdeen rushed forward before the griffins could change their minds. The magical beasts stayed perfectly still while the ghouls climbed onto their backs. The griffin's sleek feathers slid through Draculaura's fingers like water, but she held on as tightly as she could.

Then, without warning, the griffins' impossibly powerful wings began to beat—and they all lifted into the sky! Draculaura felt as if her heart were thundering even louder than the griffin's wings. With dizzying speed, the griffins spiraled into the sky, until the white sand and crystal-blue waters were a swirling blur beneath them. Draculaura buried her face in the griffin's velvet-soft feathers. But she couldn't hide her eyes for more than a few seconds. Riding a griffin was nerve-racking—but Draculaura didn't want to miss a minute of the thrilling ride!

And Draculaura was glad that she found the courage to keep her eyes open. The view was spectacular as the griffins flew the ghouls far over groves of gnarled olive trees and vineyards filled with lush green vines and dark purple grapes. The natural landscape wasn't the only impressive view, though. There were white-stone ruins—temples and amphitheaters—that Draculaura would've loved to explore, if only they had more time.

But Cleo was right: The ghouls needed to stay

focused on their mission. As the griffins began to descend, Draculaura felt a chill run down her skin—and it wasn't just from the setting sun and cool evening air at the top of the mount. She had a feeling that they were *very* close to Deuce. Soon, Draculaura knew, their questions would be answered...and the mystery behind Deuce's identity would be solved!

Much of the mount was covered with dry dirt and sharp rocks, but the griffins glided down to a grassy clearing dotted with tiny white wildflowers. Draculaura's legs were shaky as she dismounted, but she tried to steady herself as she turned to her griffin. "Thank you," she said, staring into its glittering gold eyes. "You'll never know how much you helped us."

The griffin nodded its head in response. Then, just as suddenly as they'd arrived, the griffins lifted into the air. They disappeared behind a row of gathering storm-gray clouds.

"Which way to the ruins?" Cleo asked, all business.

"I'm pretty sure it's that way," Frankie replied, gesturing to the far side of the large mount. "We're actually at the lower end of the elevation, and from the beach it looked like the columns had been built at the upper end."

"So what you're saying is, we should've packed our hiking boots?" asked Clawdeen.

"Probably," Frankie replied with a smile. "But I think we can manage without them."

"Let's get moving," Draculaura urged them. It was getting dark, and she didn't like the look of those storm clouds. She did *not* want to get stuck on this mountain in the dark, in a storm!

Plus, they were *so close*—Draculaura could feel it. The other ghouls could too. Everybody was chatting and giggling as they hurried along the twisting path, stepping over the stones and roots that jutted into the path.

"No offense to Deuce, but it looks like he could really use a landscaper up here," Clawdeen said as she shoved a particularly large rock out of the path. "This path is practically impossible to follow."

"Maybe it's intentional," Frankie suggested.

"Like booby traps?" asked Draculaura curiously.

"Not exactly...though I guess that's a possibility," Frankie replied. "What I meant was that maybe Deuce made the path so hard to follow for his protection, like from Cerberus and other beasts."

"Cerberus wasn't that bad, though," Clawdeen said. "He was really just an overgrown puppy once you got to know him."

"Right...but what about all the other Greek beasties we haven't even met yet?" Draculaura asked.

"Ghouls—check it out," Cleo said suddenly.

Is it Deuce? Draculaura thought. She looked in

the direction Cleo was pointing and discovered that they had reached the entrance to a remarkable place. It was almost like a garden, except for one big difference: It didn't have any plants. Instead, it was filled with unusual statues of people and animals. There were dozens of statues—maybe even hundreds!

"Incredible! A statuary!" Draculaura exclaimed.

"A what?" asked Clawdeen.

"A statuary is, like, a collection of statues or sculptures," Draculaura explained. "I read about it in one of my books about ancient Greece. Sculpture was a really popular art form back then."

"I think they're made of marble," Frankie said, taking a closer look at a statue of a fawn near her. "But they're so lifelike! They almost look real."

"Yeah, except for the whole frozen-in-place, made-of-cold-hard-stone thing," Clawdeen joked.

"Do you think Deuce *makes* them?" Cleo asked suddenly.

"My mom would freak if he was a sculptor. She'd love to teach somebody who's into sculpting," Clawdeen said. "But some of these are kind of…well…I don't know how to describe it."

"Weird?" Frankie suggested. "I mean, look at their faces. They look a little freaked out!"

"And those poses—like they're surprised by something," Draculaura said thoughtfully.

"Personally, I think it's really cool that Deuce has a sensitive, artistic side," Cleo said. She pulled out her phone and posed with one of the statues to take a selfie.

"If these are Deuce's creations, I bet my dad would love some in the Monster High gardens," Draculaura said. She decided to snap a pic too so she could show them to her father when the ghouls returned to Monster High.

Cleo, already leading the way, started walking faster. The path twisted and turned through the statuary until it met a tall hedge. "*Oooh—* maybe this leads to a maze!" Cleo called over her shoulder.

Hope not, Draculaura thought. They'd been slowed down enough—and getting lost in a maze of bushes was not exactly in the schedule.

Cleo disappeared behind the hedge. Draculaura frowned a little. She knew Cleo was excited to meet Deuce, but she didn't think the ghouls should split up.

"Cleo!" she called. "Wait up."

There was no answer.

Draculaura, Frankie, and Clawdeen started to run. They caught up with Cleo just as she turned the tight corner. In the center of the garden, there was a clearing that had stone benches scattered throughout it.

A manster sat on one with his back to the ghouls. Even from behind, they could tell it was Deuce right away from his hat and his sleeveless vest.

"Deuce!" Cleo called happily.

The manster turned around in surprise—and locked eyes with Cleo. A flash of green light filled the clearing.

"Cleo?" Draculaura cried urgently. "Cleo!"

But there was no response.

CHAPTER 9

Oh no! Not again!" shouted Deuce, speaking for the first time. He covered his face and hid behind a statue.

Draculaura jumped in front of Cleo, waving her hands in front of her face. "Hello? *Hello!* Answer me!" she said. "What's wrong, Cleo?"

"I can explain," Deuce said, sounding helpless and hopeless at the same time.

But Draculaura was concerned only with Cleo.

Something was wrong—very, very wrong. Cleo's regal features were frozen as though she were about to speak. In a panic, Draculaura grabbed her shoulders, hoping a good shake would snap her out of it. But Draculaura realized that her shoulders were as stiff as stone.

"*What* happened to my best ghoulfriend?" she demanded of Deuce.

"I can explain," Deuce replied from behind the statue. "But I need to stay hidden to keep the rest of you ghouls safe."

Draculaura, Frankie, and Clawdeen looked at one another in confusion. *Safe?* What did Deuce mean by that?

"I—I didn't expect anyone to come," Deuce began. "I didn't think anyone would be able to get here so quickly, which is why I wasn't extra careful."

"Well, we had one, uh, *determined* ghoul leading the pack," noted Clawdeen with a look toward the frozen Cleo. It was hard to tease her ghoul-friend while she was all statue-like. "Wanna tell us what this is about?"

Deuce sighed. "So my full name is Deuce Gorgon…My mom is Medusa," he told the ghouls. "You may have heard of her."

"Medusa!" Frankie exclaimed. "Your mom is *Medusa?*"

"The one and only," Deuce said. Without seeing his face, it was impossible to tell—but Draculaura got the feeling he was *not* very happy about it.

"I read all about her!" Frankie continued. "She's, like, *legendary!* With her snake hair and, oh man, the way she can turn anything to stone just by *looking* at it—"

Too late, Frankie realized what she had said—and what had happened to Cleo. Her pale green skin went even paler. "I—you—uh—" she stammered

Deuce pulled off his hat and peeked the back of his head out from behind the statue, revealing shiny green scales and a Mohawk made of hissing snakes! The ghouls gasped in surprise.

"Let's just say I inherited some of Mom's more infamous qualities," he said.

"But—Cleo—" Draculaura had trouble saying the words aloud.

"No, no," Deuce said quickly. "Don't worry! Your friend's going to be okay. See, I'm only *half* Gorgon. Sure, I can turn people to stone…but only for twenty-four hours—*max*. It's more of a giant inconvenience than a curse, really. I promise Cleo's going to be okay!"

The ghouls shuffled their feet uncomfortably. They were still worried about Cleo, but they also knew Deuce didn't mean to do anything bad.

"It could be worse," Deuce said self-consciously. "Full Gorgons, like Mom, turn people to stone *forever*. I'm sure you saw her collection on your way in…"

"You mean…all those statues…They used to be *alive?*" asked Draculaura.

"Bad, isn't it?" Deuce said. "I'm so careful. I do everything I can to keep others away. Cerberus at the stairs, the obstacles in the path...And I always try to avoid looking directly at anyone. Even, like, bugs. But every once in a while, if I get surprised or startled..."

Deuce didn't need to finish his sentence. The ghouls understood perfectly.

"That's why I asked you for help, actually," he said. "I'd *love* to go to Monster High. You can imagine what it's like around here. Boring...lonely. But how can I go to Monster High with this...curse?" Deuce asked. "No matter how careful I try to be, accidents happen. I know exactly how it will go down: The first time I accidentally freeze someone, that will be the end. Everyone will avoid me; I'll have exactly zero friends..."

"Not necessarily!" Draculaura said. "Everybody at Monster High knows what it's like. We all get it."

"Maybe," Deuce said. "But nobody wants to turn into a statue. Even if it lasts only for a day."

No one could disagree with him.

"I shouldn't have bothered you," Deuce said. "Messaging you was a big mistake, Draculaura. I'm sorry I reached out at all. It was stupid to think I could fit in anywhere. Not when my powers can cause trouble at any time, for anyone."

"Hey!" Draculaura protested. "Don't talk like that. We're not giving up on you. We're just getting started. Right, ghouls?"

"Right," Frankie and Clawdeen agreed.

"There *has* to be a solution...a way for you to attend Monster High without putting the other students at risk. We just haven't figured it out yet," Draculaura continued.

On the bench, Deuce sat up a little straighter—but he still didn't turn around. "You really think so?" he asked.

"I *know* so," Draculaura promised. "We just

need to go back to Monster High to figure it all out. If there's anywhere we can figure out a solution to your...situation, it's Monster High."

"Now we just need to figure out how to transport Cleo..." Frankie spoke up. "We can't just abandon her here."

"Of course not!" Draculaura replied at once. "Even if she is a statue, she's still our Cleo."

"What about the Monster Mapalogue?" Clawdeen said. "Will it work if Cleo can't put her fingers on the Skullette?"

Draculaura paused. She hadn't thought about that. "Well, I guess there's one way to find out," she said.

Then she turned back to Deuce. "Don't go anywhere," she said. "We'll be back tomorrow. I promise."

"Thanks, Draculaura," Deuce said. "And I'm sorry about your friend."

The ghouls all surrounded Statue Cleo as Draculaura pressed the Skullette against Cleo's cold, motionless hand. Then everyone else rested their fingers on it too.

Draculaura took a deep breath. Would it work? There was only one way to find out.

"Monster High. Exsto monstrum!"

CHAPTER 10

Everything went black. Draculaura shut her eyes—an instinct due more to the intense speed than the sudden darkness. A *whoooosh* filled her ears, the sound of her heart beating faster, furiously pumping her blood. Or was it the sound of travel by Mapalogue?

There was no time to think about such questions; in a blink, Draculaura hit the floor, hard. She groaned from the force of the impact and rolled onto her side. She recognized her location at once: the Libury of Monster High, the same place from which they'd departed so many hours before. Had it been just hours? Somehow it felt like days. Weeks, even.

That's when Draculaura realized how *tired* she was. It was late—later than she thought, judging from the height of the moon and the surprising quiet of the Monster High campus. But there was no time for a nap, or even a rest, not when Cleo—

"Cleo!" Draculaura gasped, suddenly remembering everything. Had the Monster Mapalogue transported Cleo in her statue form too? Or had she been left behind in Greece? Or—even worse—lost somewhere along the way?

"She's here," Clawdeen said, her voice strained. "I—*oof*—I think she kind of landed on me and now I'm stuck. Help!"

Draculaura and Frankie scrambled to their feet to lift Statue Cleo off Clawdeen's legs. Clawdeen breathed a sigh of relief as she rubbed her shins. "Thanks, ghouls," she said gratefully. "That feels a lot better."

"I'm so glad we're all here—and all in one piece," Draculaura exclaimed. She examined Statue Cleo for nicks or chips, but didn't spot a single one. Even her nail polish was pristine!

"I'm glad the Mapalogue left us *here*—and not in the middle of the Creepeteria," Frankie said. "Can you imagine what everybody would've said if we suddenly showed up with Statue Cleo?"

"Nightmare!" Draculaura agreed. "We've got to keep this whole statue thing on the down low. I love Cleo, and I know she'll be back to normal soon...but Statue Cleo is kind of *eerie* looking."

"We can't just leave her here, though," Clawdeen said. "What if someone comes into the Libury to do some homework? Or just find a book to read?"

"So what are we gonna do?" asked Frankie. "Hide her in the closet?"

"Ghoul! Of course not!" Draculaura exclaimed. "Cleo would never forgive us if we shoved her in a dusty closet!"

Frankie raised an eyebrow. "Do *you* have a better idea?" she replied.

"Um…" Draculaura said, stalling as she tried to think of something—*anything*. "Uh…I guess we have to figure out the safest place for Cleo. A place where nobody will accidentally discover her. Maybe we should take her to my dorm room!"

"But that's up, like, five flights of stairs!" Clawdeen said.

"With the three of us, we can totally manage it!" Draculaura said encouragingly. "Come on, ghouls! We'll just walk her up the stairs and pretend like we're all whispering to her or something. No one will notice a thing!"

"It's worth a try," Frankie said. "The sooner we get Cleo safely hidden, the sooner we can start solving Deuce's problem."

It was a good plan—in theory. But in reality, it was a lot harder to maneuver Statue Cleo than Draculaura and her ghoulfriends had anticipated. Every time they pulled her onto a new stair, the statue made a hollow *thunk* that reverberated throughout the entire staircase! Whispering wasn't going to work. The ghouls would have to be a lot louder if they wanted to drown out the clunking noise.

"Start laughing right now," Draculaura hissed at Frankie and Clawdeen.

"Huh?" Frankie asked.

"Pretend you just heard something hilarious and laugh your head off," Draculaura explained. "Not literally, though," she added to Frankie.

"I get it. If we're laughing loud enough, then no one will hear Cleo thunking up the stairs," Clawdeen said.

"Exactly," Draculaura replied. "Hahaha! Ha ha, ha-ha-ha-ha!"

Thunk.

"Ha ha ha ha ha!"

Thunk.

"Ha ha ha ha ha ha!"

By this point, Draculaura was desperate to reach her room! She couldn't tell if they were attracting even more attention now. Luckily, there were just five more steps—four—three—two—one—and at last the ghouls hurried Statue Cleo into the room. Draculaura was so relieved to be there that she slammed the door behind them.

"We made it," she said, breathing a sigh of relief. "And I don't think anyone suspects a thing!"

Just then, the door crashed open with a loud *bang!* Draculaura and her friends screamed before they realized it was only Lagoona.

"Ghouls! You're back! Tryouts went *great*! I'm sure we're going to have the best team in no time. But let me tell you, my fins are *still* sore...uh, why are you all cowering in the corner?"

Catching her breath, Draculaura spoke up. "You scared us!" she said at last, pressing her hand over her heart.

"How did you know we were back, Lagoona?" asked Frankie.

"I heard your laughter echoing all the way to the pool," she replied. "That must have been some rescue! So where's Deuce? Is he settling in? Cleo, what did you—"

Lagoona's voice trailed off abruptly. "What's wrong with Cleo?" she asked.

"Um…it's not as bad as it seems," Clawdeen began. "She kind of got turned into a statue—"

"A statue?" Lagoona cried. "Oh no! Poor Cleo!"

"Hold on," Draculaura interrupted her. "It's not permanent. It's only going to last for a day or so. Then she'll be back to normal."

"But *how* did this happen?" Lagoona said.

Draculaura took a deep breath and told her the whole story. "So that's why Deuce didn't know if he should come to Monster High," she finished. "He was worried that he might accidentally turn students into statues."

"Yeah," Lagoona replied, eyeing the statue. "I can see why he'd be concerned."

"That's the problem we have to solve," Frankie spoke up. "How can we make it safe for Deuce to attend? How can we stop his statue stare?"

There was a long silence.

"If you ghouls have an idea, just say it," Draculaura encouraged her ghoulfriends. "Anything is a start!"

"What about…a really thick blindfold?" Clawdeen suggested.

"A blindfold?" Frankie repeated. "I guess that would keep Deuce's gaze from turning anyone to stone."

"But I'm not sure how much easier it would make his life," Lagoona mused. "I think that's the right idea, though. How do we block Deuce's gaze?"

"While still making it possible for him to see," Draculaura added.

"Blinders," Frankie said suddenly. "Horses wear blinders!"

"Huh?" asked Clawdeen.

"They're, like, screens that horses wear on the sides of their eyes," Frankie explained. "They keep a horse from seeing things to the side, so it won't get startled. It can still see straight ahead, though, so it knows where it's going."

"So...blinders...if we could convince Deuce to wear them, would solve half the problem," Draculaura said thoughtfully. "But he can still see straight ahead—which means anyone who crosses his path would be at risk for becoming a statue."

Saying those words out loud made Draculaura realize just how serious Deuce's situation was. She wondered for a minute what her dad would say if he knew what was going on. Dracula was as committed to Monster High as his daughter—but he had to consider the safety of all the students. They'd never had a scenario in which one monster posed a serious threat to the others… until now.

I have to tell Dad, Draculaura realized with a sinking feeling. *I can't just bring Deuce here without letting Dad know what's going on. But maybe—hopefully—we can come up with a plan first. If there was a way to…*

Suddenly, Draculaura gasped. She'd figured it out! She'd solved the problem!

"What is it?" Frankie asked.

"Cleo!" Draculaura cried out. "Since before we even left for Greece!"

"What are you talking about?" Clawdeen asked, confused.

Draculaura ran to Statue Cleo and reached

into her pocket. She pulled out a folded-up piece of paper and cheered in triumph. "Yes!" she cried. "Cleo had the answer—even before we knew the problem!"

Draculaura unfolded the paper and held up Cleo's drawing for custom sunglasses. "Remember Cleo's sunglasses idea? The ones with the reflective lenses? She wanted to make a pair for each one of us—but we really just need a pair for Deuce!" she exclaimed.

"Genius!" Lagoona cried.

"What do you think, Frankie?" Draculaura asked. "Do you think it will work?"

Frankie took the sketch from Draculaura and studied it, concentrating so hard that a frown flickered across her face. "They couldn't be just ordinary mirrored lenses," she finally said. "They'd have to be thicker than usual...possibly with some kind of special coating on both sides to absorb the power of Deuce's gaze..."

"But is it possible?" Draculaura said. "Can you invent it?"

"I don't know," Frankie said. "But I can try!"

"Tell us exactly how we can help," Clawdeen said.

"Yeah!" Draculaura added. "You'll have a whole team of lab assistants at your disposal!"

Frankie grinned at her ghoulfriends. "Okay, team," she announced. "Let's get to work!"

🐍 🐍 🐍

For the next several hours, the five ghouls holed up in the Mad Science lab. There was a lot more involved in making a pair of sunglasses than the ghouls would've guessed. First, Frankie showed them how to make a mold for the frame. "We want it to be bigger than an ordinary sunglasses frame," she explained. "That way, we'll lower the chance that Deuce might accidentally glance at someone from outside the frame."

"Now what?" asked Clawdeen once the mold was ready.

"Now it's Mad Scientist time!" Frankie joked. "We're going to combine a bunch of chemicals into a polymer plastic. What color did Cleo use for Deuce's glasses again?"

"Red," Draculaura reported.

After the ghouls mixed the polymer, Frankie carefully poured it into the mold. "We'll let this sit until the frame is hardened. In the meantime, we can make the lenses—and figure out the best way to polarize them."

The night grew later and later as Frankie cut and polished a pair of lenses for Deuce's new shades. Then came the tricky part: inventing a new formula for coating the lenses. Despite the bright lights of the lab, first Lagoona, then Clawdeen dozed off. Draculaura did everything she could to stay awake, stifling one giant yawn after another, but her eyelids felt heavier…and heavier…

"How's the formula coming?" she asked Frankie sleepily.

"I don't know," Frankie replied, sighing. "I have this double-dip process to coat both sides of the lenses, but we won't know if it's enough until Deuce tries them on…and tests them out."

"Pretty high stakes," Draculaura remarked.

"Exactly," Frankie said. "Maybe too high."

Draculaura picked up one of the coated lenses and held it up to her lavender eye. She took a closer look at the lens, tilting it this way and that under the bright lights of the lab. At some angles, she could see faint, vertical lines from the coating Frankie had applied.

"What if…" Draculaura began. Deep in thought, her voice trailed off.

"What if what?" Frankie prompted her.

"What if you applied the coating from, like, different angles?" Draculaura said. "So it criss-crossed like a web?"

Frankie stared at the lens too. "Different layers of coating, interlocking for maximum light—or curse—absorbency?" she said.

"Yeah, what you said," Draculaura replied.

"You know what, Drac?" Frankie asked.

"What?"

"You're a genius!"

And without another word, Frankie picked up her brush and started coating the lenses in all different directions. Draculaura leaned back, smiled, and yawned. The ghouls didn't know if their plan would work—but Draculaura knew that they'd done everything possible to make it succeed.

🐍　🐍　🐍

The ghouls awoke bright and early the next morning while the rest of the students were still asleep.

"The mold!" Frankie cried. "Oh, I hope it set overnight!"

The ghouls held their breaths while Frankie eased the sunglasses frame out of the mold. To their delight, it was solid—and the lenses she'd made were a perfect fit!

"All right!" cheered Clawdeen. "Now let's grab Cleo and get back to Greece!"

"Hang on a minute," Draculaura spoke up.

The other ghouls turned to look at her.

"We have to tell my dad what's been going on," she said.

"What if he doesn't let you go back to Greece?" Lagoona asked.

"That's a risk we have to take," Draculaura explained. "Besides, if he found out that I kept something *this* important a secret, he would probably never let us go on another rescue mission again."

No one spoke for a moment, but Draculaura

could tell from the expressions on the other ghouls' faces that they knew she was right.

"I know my dad can seem kind of, well, over-protective," she continued. "But I can't keep a secret from him if it means I'll lose his trust."

"Okay, then," Frankie said. "Let's go tell Mr. D."

The ghouls found him in the Creepeteria, enjoying a pot of bat tea before the rest of the school was awake.

"Morning, ghouls," Dracula said, sounding way too chipper for so early in the morning. "How's the rescue mission?"

"Hopefully nearing a successful ending," Draculaura began. Then she told him everything—Cerberus, the griffins, the statuary, and Deuce's dangerous stare. Dracula's face grew more and more troubled, but Draculaura didn't leave out a single detail.

"So Deuce is a Gorgon descendent," Dracula said when his daughter finished. "Remarkable. To be honest, I haven't thought much about how we will handle our more, uh, *exciting* students."

"You'll let him come to Monster High, won't you?" asked Draculaura. She thrust the special sunglasses across the table. "At least let us try the shades and see if they work. It just wouldn't be fair for Deuce to be stuck all alone on that island!"

"And it wouldn't be fair to put all our other students at risk, either," Dracula said gently. "Don't you think Cleo would agree?"

"Not necessarily," Draculaura argued. "Cleo was more eager to rescue Deuce than anyone. And she's the one who figured out a way to solve the problem—even before she knew what the real problem was!"

"And there may be more than one solution," Dracula mused.

Draculaura's heart fluttered. Was her dad about to give in?

"Here's the deal," he continued. "You can go

back to Greece and give Deuce the glasses. Have him test them out—on an ant or a fly, *not* on one of you. If they work, bring him back."

"And if they *don't* work?" asked Draculaura anxiously.

Dracula's face wrinkled in concern. "I'll need to have a faculty meeting with the teachers before we can officially enroll Deuce," he said. "We may need to make some preparations before we can accommodate him, but we'll make it work somehow."

"Thanks, Dad," Draculaura whispered as she gave him a hug. "We'll be back as soon as we can." *Hopefully, with Deuce,* she thought—but she didn't say the words aloud.

"I know you will," Dracula replied. "And, Drac?"

"Be careful?" she guessed.

"Be *extra* careful," he said.

CHAPTER 11

The ghouls raced off to Draculaura's room, grabbed on to Statue Cleo, and waited for Draculaura to say the magic words. Before she did, Draculaura made sure—one more time—that the special glasses were safely stored in her pocket. Then, once she knew that all her ghoulfriends were touching the Skullette, she said all in a rush, *"Deuce. Exsto monstrum!"*

Whooooooosh!

Seconds later, Draculaura found herself blinking on that same white sandy beach. The ghouls were right back where they'd started, near the carved stone stairs set into the mount—but this time, Cerberus was nowhere in sight. Draculaura was secretly thrilled—she'd grown to like the ginormous puppy, but she already knew they'd have enough trouble getting Statue Cleo up the stone stairs without having to play with Cerberus first.

"On my count," Draculaura said. "One, two, three, *lift*." And carefully, gradually, they carried Statue Cleo up every step. It was easier to lift the statue with Lagoona along to help.

The sun was just rising over the mount when the ghouls reached the top. They were much closer to Deuce than they'd been after the griffins had dropped them off; Draculaura could see the statue garden just a few feet away and the thick green hedge just beyond it. She smiled to herself.

Always trust the Monster Mapalogue, she thought. *It knows exactly where we need to go.*

The ghouls were unusually quiet as they approached the hedges. No one wanted to sneak up on Deuce accidentally—or startle him—after what had happened to Cleo. But it was impossible to know where he was.

"Should we—I don't know—make a lot of noise?" asked Clawdeen.

"I know!" Frankie said. "Does anybody have a mirror?"

"Of course," Draculaura and Clawdeen replied.

"But you look *fangtastic*, ghoul—no need for a touch-up," added Draculaura.

Frankie grinned. "That's not why I asked," she said. "Watch this!"

Frankie snapped open their compacts and showed the ghouls how to use the mirrors to peek around corners—so they could see if Deuce was there *before* they made a move.

"Good thinking, Frankie," Draculaura said. "Want me to take the lead?"

"Sure," Frankie replied as she passed the mirrors to Drac. "Don't worry about Cleo. Clawdeen, Lagoona, and I will carry her."

Draculaura took cautious steps, past each hedge, along the twisting and turning passageway, until she reached the clearing where they'd found Deuce yesterday. She remembered all too well what had happened when Cleo, in her excitement, had charged forward.

"Deuce?" Draculaura called, pressing herself against the hedge. "We're back. Are you there?"

"I'm here!" he replied. "My eyes are covered. It's safe."

Draculaura breathed a sigh of relief as she entered the clearing. Deuce was sitting on a bench, his head in his hands. She knew it was for her protection, but the sight filled her with pity. If the sunglasses *didn't* work—if she had to tell him that he had to stay behind again until her dad and the other teachers could come up with a plan—

Draculaura shook her head, hoping to send the thoughts out of her mind. *The glasses will work,* she told herself. *They have to.*

"You came back!" Deuce said.

"Of course we came back!" Draculaura said. "We promised, didn't we?"

"I just…wasn't sure," Deuce admitted. "I know it's a lot to risk. The thought of being turned into a statue and all. How's your cute friend—*ahem*—I mean, your friend? Your regular friend…the, uh, one I turned into a statue?"

The ghouls shot one another a knowing look and shared a smile.

"Oh, Cleo's just about the same," reported Frankie. "Still a statue, but it hasn't been twenty-four hours yet—"

"She'll wake up! I promise," Deuce interrupted. "My powers aren't *that* strong."

"So…we had an idea," Draculaura began. "It was Cleo's idea, actually, before she became a… well, never mind, it's kind of a long story, and I'm sure you're—"

"What Drac's *trying* to say," Clawdeen said, cutting off Draculaura's awkward explanation, "is that we made you some stylin' shades."

"Super-special sunglasses," Lagoona added. "With custom lenses."

"Custom lenses?" Deuce repeated, his curiosity piqued.

"The lenses have a unique coating that consists of interlocking lines that—oh, you know what, who cares about the science? Let's just see if they work!" Frankie said.

Draculaura crept forward and placed them on the bench next to Deuce. He didn't turn his head to look at her, not even a fraction of an inch. "Our hope is that they'll absorb whatever it is in your gaze that turns others into statues," she said. "But…we need to make sure they work."

He pulled on the sunglasses and said, "Nice. I guess I should…"

At the same moment, he and Draculaura spotted a caterpillar inching along the bench. Draculaura held her breath as Deuce turned his head. She could see his face in profile…could even see the way his eyes flashed with green light—the same green light she'd seen when Cleo had been statue-fied—

But the caterpillar kept inching along.

And the green light?

It was instantly absorbed into the lenses—just as Frankie had planned.

"It worked!" Deuce yelled, his voice filled with shock and amazement. "Look—the caterpillar—it's fine—totally fine!"

Then all the ghouls were happily screaming

and cheering too, and Deuce turned around to look at them and flashed the most dazzling grin.

"What—what happened?" Cleo's voice, oddly sleepy, rang out. She stretched her arms and yawned before she suddenly remembered where they were. She stood up a little taller, her shoulders a little straighter.

"Cleo!" Draculaura cried. "You're—you're—*you* again!"

"Of course I'm me," Cleo said. "What are you talking about?"

But all the ghouls were too busy laughing and hugging to answer her.

"We'll tell you everything later," Draculaura promised. "In the meantime, there's someone I'd like you to meet. This is Deuce Gorgon. Deuce, Cleo is, like, the reason that everything's worked out so well."

Deuce gave Cleo a brilliant smile. "Hey, Cleo," he said. "How can I ever thank you?"

Was it Draculaura's imagination—or did Cleo's cheeks turn a tiny bit pink? *It's probably just the sunrise*, she thought as beautiful light spilled over the hedges.

"Grab your stuff," Clawdeen said to Deuce. "If we hurry, we can make it back to Monster High in time for breakfast."

Cleo leaned close to Draculaura's ear. "Deuce seems *really* nice," she whispered. "I kind of wish he'd take off the shades, though. I'd love to gaze deep into his eyes!"

Draculaura started to laugh. "Trust me, ghoulfriend," she said. "That's the *last* thing you want!"

Did you 🖤 reading about
Deuce Gorgon's rescue?
Then you'll love

**TURN THE PAGE
FOR A SNEAK PEEK!**

CHAPTER 1

hoosh!

Draculaura steadied herself, and then she reached out a hand to make sure her newest ghoulfriend, Lagoona Blue, didn't stumble as the Monster Mapalogue dropped them in the grass right outside Monster High. But with years of experience surfing, Lagoona was ready for the unexpected landing. Even though she'd spent most of her time in the crystal-blue waters of the Great Barrier Reef, Lagoona was surprisingly steady on dry land!

Draculaura snuck a sideways glance at Lagoona as the sea ghoul shielded her eyes and stared up at the building looming ahead of them. *I wish I knew what she was thinking*, Draculaura thought. The moment when a monster set eyes on Monster High for the very first time always filled her with nervous expectation.

But there was no need for Draculaura to worry. An enormous smile spread across Lagoona's pale-blue face. "Crikey!" she exclaimed. "It's fintastic!"

"Yay!" Draculaura squealed as she clapped her hands together. "I'm so happy you are here!"

Nearby, Draculaura's other ghoulfriends—Clawdeen Wolf, Frankie Stein, and Cleo de Nile—picked themselves up and peeled off the special wetsuits they'd designed to find Lagoona in the Great Barrier Reef.

"*Ahhh*, it's so good to be home," Clawdeen sighed happily as she squeezed salt water out of her thick hair.

Home. That was what Draculaura had called the sprawling mansion her entire life. In fact, she'd never known anything different. Ever since the great monster Fright Flight, Draculaura and her father, Dracula, had been in hiding from humans (or "Normies," as they were known in the monster world). It had been just the two of them, century after century, in the rambling mansion. It wasn't the worst life—Draculaura loved her dad a lot, and she always had fun fanging out with her pet spider, Webby—but it could get lonely. Really lonely. More than anything, Draculaura had longed for ghoulfriends her own age. But how could she ever meet a new ghoulfriend when she had to hide from everyone?

Then, on the night of her first flying lesson, *everything* changed. Draculaura met Frankie, and they had the brilliant idea to transform Draculaura's home into Monster High: a school where monsters could finally come out of the shadows and just be themselves! It had taken a lot of planning—and a *lot* of work—but at last, Monster High was just about ready to open. Draculaura and her ghoulfriends had been working overtime to track down new students for Monster High. Frankie and Clawdeen had been living nearby, but there was a whole wide world of lonely monsters who longed for friends, just like Draculaura had. With the help of the Monster Mapalogue, Draculaura, Frankie, and Clawdeen had traveled far and wide to find and rescue Cleo and Lagoona. From fighting mummies in the cursed tombs of Egypt's deserts to surviving a massive tropical cyclone in the Great Barrier Reef, Draculaura wasn't just excited to be back at Monster High; she was relieved. It felt *fangtastic* to be home!

Draculaura reached out to link arms with Lagoona. "What do you think?" she asked. "Ready for the grand tour?"

Lagoona flicked her long blonde-and-blue hair

over her scaly shoulder. "You know it, ghoul!" she said in her bubbly, upbeat way that made everyone want to be her new best ghoulfriend. "But, just wondering, do you have a pool?"

Draculaura put her hands on her hips and pretended to be outraged. "Do you *really* think I'd bring you all the way here just to leave you totally landlocked?" she asked—but the twinkle in her eyes told everyone she was just joking.

Lagoona started to laugh, and the other ghouls joined in. "It's going to be a big change, and I'm ready to ride the wave," she replied. "I'm lucky— since I'm a sea monster, I can manage on land *and* in the water. But I have to admit, I'd miss the chance to start each day with a swim and a stroll along the shore."

"We're not quite ready to offer you a sandy beach," Clawdeen spoke up, "but there is a pool!"

"It's where Clawdeen taught me how to swim!" Cleo chimed in. Her golden chandelier earrings gleamed in the sunlight. "And it's where I *daringly* tested out Frankie's new wetsuit before we came to rescue you!"

"Sounds positively fintastic," Lagoona replied.

"Getting you settled in will be top priority," Clawdeen promised as the ghoulfriends began the short walk up the Hill to Monster High.

"Unless we need to set off on another urgent monster-rescue mission," Cleo added.

"Yeah, about that…" Draculaura began.

Everyone turned to look at her.

"Maybe we should finish getting Monster High ready before we start searching for more students," Draculaura suggested. "Think about it—there are five of us now. If we keep going at this pace, we'll have full enrollment before you know it. What will we do with all the monsters we rescue?"

"*Hmmm*," Clawdeen replied. "I hadn't thought of it like that before."

"Don't you think any ghouls or goblins who contact us would rather be *here*, at an unfinished Monster High, than stuck where they are?" Cleo pointed out. "I mean, I was becoming *totally unwrapped* in my tomb for that millennium. It was phenomenally boring! I can say with full confidence that I'd *much* rather be here, helping out, than there, bored out of my mind."

"That's a good point," Draculaura admitted. "I hate to make any monsters wait even one day longer than they absolutely have to."

"I've got an idea," Frankie announced. "Since we don't have any monsters waiting on us right now, we can all just get to work on Monster High! We'll focus on finishing every important thing that still needs attention, and if we receive any really urgent calls, we can go get our ghoul."

"Sounds like a plan," Draculaura said. "I'm going to the Howl of History! It's in need of some serious organization."

"Not to mention some serious *dusting*," Cleo added, making a face.

"Those books might have a thousand years' worth of dust on them," Draculaura replied with a laugh. "Dad's never been the best with the feather duster."

"You're coming with me," Frankie told Lagoona. "I want you to check out the pool and let me know if we need to make any modifications so it feels just like home."

"Thanks, ghoulfriend," Lagoona said gratefully. "I really appreciate it!"

Draculaura turned to Clawdeen and Cleo. "What about you two?" she asked. "Any ideas?"

"Schedules!" Clawdeen and Cleo replied at the same time. The two ghouls turned to each other in surprise.

"I have to admit, I'm kind of surprised," said Clawdeen. "I didn't know you were interested in class schedules too."

Cleo's blue eyes grew as wide as the gems in her bejeweled headband. "Oh no, not at *all*," she assured Clawdeen. "I'm talking about extracurricular schedules. You know: clubs, sports, teams—the fun stuff!"

Draculaura laughed again. "I think it's all going to be fun, once Monster High is really up and running," she said. "Come on, let's grab some Mummy Mochas and get to work!"

*   *   *

An hour later, Draculaura found herself in the deserted Howl of History. She'd taken a quick detour to her bedroom to pick up her pet spider, Webby, for some company—and some extra help too.

Draculaura had been to the Howl of History before when she was searching for clues to rescue Cleo, but that didn't lessen her sense of wonder as she gazed at the enchanted maps and ancient volumes of monster lore that lined the walls. "It's so fangtastic," Draculaura said in awe.

Then she sneezed so loudly that she kicked up a cloud of dust!

"Whoops!" Draculaura giggled as she waved her hand in front of her face. "Sorry, Webby," she added as the little spider sneezed too. "I guess Cleo was right; it is pretty dusty in here! But not for long…let's do this thing!"

Draculaura quickly checked her iCoffin to make sure she didn't have any missed messages before she put her full concentration into organizing the Howl of History's shelves. *All clear to clean!* she thought to herself as she put aside her phone, rolled up her sleeves, and got right to work. She started dusting the highest bookshelves so that eventually all the dust would fall to the floor. Even Webby pitched in, shooting strands of his sticky spiderweb across the room to trap itty-bitty specks of dust.

"Not bad—*achoo!*—huh?" Draculaura asked through a sneezing attack. "Once we—*achoo!*—mop the—*achoo!*—floors—"

Crash!

Draculaura froze mid-sneeze.

At the far end of the Howl of History, there was an ancient text lying on the floor. A creepy feeling crawled down Draculaura's spine. She was *certain* that book hadn't been there just moments ago.

"It's probably no big deal," Draculaura said slowly. Her voice echoed through the room. "Maybe it just fell…when I was dusting…on the other side of the room…"

Crash!

This time, Draculaura didn't need to speculate. She just saw another book fly off the very same shelf with her own two vampire eyes!

The sight was so alarming that in a split second, Draculaura had transformed into a bat. She had one goal and one goal only: grab Webby and fly as far from this haunted Howl of History as she possibly could. She had a terrible feeling that someone—or *something*—was making those books fly off the shelves. There couldn't possibly be another explanation.

Or could there?